# THE CHRISTMAS ANGEL OF THE NORTH

A festive mini treat!

Kimberley Adams

**Shy Bairns Publishing**

Copyright © 2024 Kimberley Adams

The right of Kimberley Adams to be identified as the author of this work has been asserted in accordance with the Copyright, Designs and Patents Act 1988.
All rights reserved. No part of this publication may be reproduced, stored in or transmitted into any retrieval system, in any form, or by any means (electronic, mechanical, photocopying, recording or otherwise) without the prior written permission of the publisher. Any person who does any unauthorised act in relation to this publication may be liable to criminal prosecution and civil claims for damages.
This is a work of fiction. Names, characters, businesses, places, events and incidents are either the products of the author's imagination or used in a fictitious manner. Any resemblance to actual persons, living or dead, or actual events is purely coincidental.

Cover design copyright © Sarah Farooqi

ISBN:978-1-7385717-1-0

*For Angels of the North everywhere!*

# CONTENTS

Title Page
Copyright
Dedication
Chapter 1   1
Chapter 2   10
Chapter 3   17
Chapter 4   23
Chapter 5   29
Chapter 6   38
Chapter 7   45
Chapter 8   54
Chapter 9   60
Chapter 10   67
Chapter 11   74
Chapter 12   79

| | |
|---|---|
| Chapter 13 | 85 |
| Chapter 14 | 93 |
| Chapter 15 | 99 |
| Chapter 16 | 104 |
| Chapter 17 | 112 |
| Chapter 18 | 118 |
| Chapter 19 | 125 |
| Chapter 20 | 131 |
| Chapter 21 | 140 |
| Afterword | 149 |
| Thank you... | 151 |
| Praise For Author | 153 |
| Books By This Author | 155 |
| Social Media Links | 157 |

# CHAPTER 1

'Donna, have you seen this? It's perfect for us,' said Shan, waving her phone about. Shan's my best friend, even though we are chalk and cheese, but I forgive her for being a bit dotty on the basis that having a name like Shania Twine (it's a long story) must have played havoc with her cognitive development. That and heading a few too many footballs. Mind you, my mother didn't do much better calling me Madonna after her favourite singer in all the world. I think her and Shan's mam were in cahoots, trying to outdo one another in the famous singer stakes. I quite liked my name until I got to High School when I suddenly became 'that Mad Donna Dobbs, her with the pointy boobs,' so as soon as I left the educational equivalent of Strangeways, I dropped the Mad bit and became plain old Donna Dobbs. And I'll stick with that, thank you very much.

'What is it?' I asked, dragging my eyes away from TikTok, where some woman was convincing me that by next week I could write a book and make a million quid, if I paid her fifty Crypto coins to tell me her secret. I'd wanted to be a writer for as long as I could remember, and now I had my name sorted, Donna Dobbs would look good on the spine of a book. After quite a lot of research and accusations of loitering in Waterstones, I can confirm that the initial D is a good place to be on the shelves. One day, I will find my arcs and tropes, whatever they are, and I'll become an international best seller like… like… that tall man off Pointless.

'It's an advert for Renwick's, the big department store in the town.'

'I know what Renwick's is, Shan. What're they flogging off now? Brad Balls was telling me he'd got a pair of designer trainers in there last week for half-price.'

'Lying toad!' harrumphed Shan. 'He got them from the back room of Pound Xpress in the precinct, for a fiver. Snides. He nearly gassed everyone in Betty's Baps yesterday, cos I think the plastic they're made from is toxic. Anyway, it's not that kind of advert – it's for jobs.'

At that, the door creaked open and in came my Nana Mary.

'Just thought I'd pop in on the way home. I've been to Knit and Natter – not that there's ever much knitting goes on – today's hot topic of conversation was Dolly Dixon's bowels.'

Shan and I looked at each other in horror, having heard far too much about the gastric gurglings of half of Lockley's pensioners.

'She ate too many prunes and apparently it was the colour of *Grizzly Bear*.'

'Grizzly what?' I raised an eyebrow, realising that I would probably live to regret asking.

'You know, like on those fancy pants paint charts,' said Nana. 'Old Joe has just painted his boudoir in *School Custard*.'

'Eww, that sounds gross,' I said.

'Eeh, I loved school custard. But the pink sort,' laughed Shan.

'I'm surprised Joe didn't go for *Pink Blancmange*,' said Nana. 'And before you tell me I'm not allowed to say things like that anymore

– blah, blah, blah, I just have, because it's true. Joe loves pink and only bought the yellow as they could hardly give it away. Anyway, back to Dolly's bowels…'

'Nana!'

'Is your mam at work? I bet she'd be interested.'

I very much doubted that.

'Anyway, budge up the settee you two,' she said, pushing her way between us. 'What kind of jobs you talking about, Shania? You two could do with something to keep you out of mischief. After you being sacked more times than a politician, Donna, it will do you good to have a focus for a change.'

Nana may have had a point. I was on a gap year, but without the benefit of exotic trips to explore new cultures – and party like a rock star. The most I got offered was two weeks in Brenda the Bag's minging caravan at Whitley Bay – it was all we could afford. I was the first in our family to go to university, and with money being tight, mam said I needed to work until the time came to start my course. Trouble was, well, trouble seemed to follow me about. I couldn't seem to keep out of it, and so far, my foray into the world of employment had been a rocky one.

'You've got a point, Nana,' I laughed. 'Remember when we nearly blinded you practicing microblading?'

'Like I'll ever forget. You nearly killed me!' said Nana dramatically.

'And then you caused havoc in Go Your Own Way,' Shan howled. 'I thought your mam must have had too many gins when she came up with that one. I mean, you, in a funeral parlour. Whatever could go wrong?' She rocked with laughter.

'Then there was Betty's Baps. I only went there for the banter to use for material for my book. It wasn't *my* fault the kitchen flooded, and Betty burned the scones. That was all down to Orange Morgan. What our Aaron sees in that overripe satsuma is beyond me,' I tutted.

'I still think your best effort was when you were supposed to be helping in Tommy the Tatts Parlour, and he gave Callum Scott that tattoo of a barbie; it even had a couple of bangers cooking and little wisps of smoke...'

'And it was meant to be a Barbie doll, wasn't it? Nana laughed.

'Yes, he wanted to impress his girlfriend, apparently. Not my fault he wasn't clear enough.'

'Well, it's time you did something without getting sacked. And I suppose you're looking for something temporary, Shania, seeing as Shirley has shut the salon while she's off on that mega cruise for her golden wedding?'

Shan was on an apprenticeship in Shirley's Salon in the precinct, but her main love was football. She was soon having a trial for the big women's club in Newcastle, having played for Lockley Lasses since she was a tot.

'Yes, I could do with something until she gets back in January, and this looks perfect,' Shan nodded. 'It's for the Christmas grotto in Renwick's, Nana Mary. They're looking for staff.'

'What kind of staff?' I raised my eyebrow.

'I'll read it out: "*Renwick's has been providing outstanding Christmas activities for over one hundred years. From our world-famous Christmas window displays to our magical grotto, where little one's gaze in wonderment as they enter Santa's*

*Cottage, Renwick's is the place to be during the festive season. Brand new for this year is our AI generated imagery in our new futuristic capsule ride to the North Pole, guaranteed to light up little faces!"'*

'Aye, and probably make them all travel sick,' I muttered. 'Imagine cleaning that up every day?'

'Shh, Donna man, I'm not finished yet.' Shan continued reading: *"Renwick's is seeking the final few performers for this very important offering in our store calendar. We require two elves, and due to our usual angel leaving us for the Theatre Royal pantomime, we now require someone to fill the especially key role of Christmas Angel of the North."'*

'There's no way I'm going to apply to be the angel. It's elf or nothing for me,' I said defiantly.

'You haven't got the right attributes to be an elf, Donna,' muttered Shan.

'What, like pointy ears and big feet you mean?'

Shan ignored me. 'Well, I can't be the angel. Howay man, Donna, can you really see me as that? Shirley's always saying I'm the spawn of the Devil, not a flipping angel. And I don't do dresses, as you well know. How many angels have you seen wearing trackies? At least if I was the elf, I might be able to wear me Doc Martens with a couple of bells stuck on the toes. Anyway, they're looking for two elves, so we can both be one. Just got to get rid of the other competition somehow.'

I snatched the phone out of Shan's hand. 'You didn't read this bit: *"Preference will be given to candidates who have experience in acting and singing."* You're having a laugh, aren't you?' I said, throwing her phone back to her. 'Acting. Singing. Us?'

'Erm, I'll just remind you: Fact. You're Madonna, and I'm Shania. With names like ours, well we've got it in the bag. Imagine the publicity Renwick's could get in the *Chronicle* telling everyone that Madonna and Shania are appearing in the grotto. And we've both watched *Elf* every year since we were about five, so I reckon with a little bit of—'

'Lying?'

'I'm thinking more being creative with the truth. We have acted… when we were in the school nativity.'

'Aye, Shan, as the front and back of a donkey. I'm still recovering from having your backside in me face. I should have been at the front, or at least we could have taken turns, but no….'

Nana, who had remained quiet throughout our discussion suddenly burst into life. 'An angel you say?' She stroked her chin, which signalled her in contemplation mode. 'Just for November through to Christmas? I could quite fancy that myself. Always been theatrical, as you well know, Donna. I can sing and dance and, well, it would be such fun us three working together.'

It was true. Nana had been in a song and dance troupe when she was young and was still theatrical to this day. But as for it being fun for us to work together, that might be stretching it! Shan and I exchanged horrified glances, our bickering having come to an abrupt ceasefire.

'You, an angel in Renwick's grotto, Nana?' I gasped.

'Yes, me, and why the blooming heck not?'

# CHAPTER 2

Nana gave us the look. The one that said, 'choose your words very carefully.'

'So, come on – why shouldn't I be the Christmas Angel of the North? I'm from the north and *nearly* everyone says I'm an angel. I think I'm perfect for the role.'

'Well, erm, just think how tiring it will be for one thing,' I said, trying to be diplomatic.

'And all those screaming kids projectile vomiting after an AI ride in what amounts to a giant bean can,' Shan shuddered.

'And you'll miss Knit and Natter... and the Bingo Club... not to mention *Bargain Hunt*,' I added.

'And you'll have to wear this,' said Shan, shoving her phone in front of us to show a picture of the angel from last year's grotto. 'I wouldn't be seen dead in that, man. Imagine the lasses on the team taking the pee!'

'And I'm not wearing that either,' I screeched as I looked at a picture of a tall, slender, dark-haired girl, who was indisputably beautiful but wearing a meringue frock that made her resemble the crinoline lady toilet roll holder in the library bogs.

'She looks like that toilet—' began Shan.

'—Roll cover in the library,' I finished the sentence for her.

'Here, old Joe made that, and we're all very fond of Julie Andrex. We've had her years.'

'Julie who?'

Nana ignored me and continued: 'Anyhow, don't know why you two don't like that dress. It's lovely – just like what a princess would wear. I'd look fabulous in it. Granted, she's a different shape to me, but I could take up the hem. And I've got some flab sucker-inner underwear from Temu. Blooming magic, it is.'

'Where does all the spare flab go to when you wear it, Nana Mary?' Shan squeaked as she sucked in air, her mouth like a raspberry, while holding her middle where no actual fat existed on her.

'China,' said Nana seriously. 'So, you two, is that the best you've got to throw at me as to why I shouldn't apply?'

'Well, I just thought it might be too much for you,' I said.

'Because I'm old? Is that what you're trying to say, Donna? Just spit it out. How old do you think I am?'

'Eigh...' began Shan, before I silenced her with a quick death stare.

'I'll have you know it starts with an S, you two. I'm nowhere near E yet. I'm in me prime – there are much older people than me working in B&Q.'

'There are, Nana Mary,' Shan nodded. 'I swear there's a man on the plumbing aisle about ninety-six. Norman. He's dead canny – gave me a free sample of Climaflex...'

'Shania, pet, are you certain you were in B&Q? I'm sure I've seen that in the Ann Summers catalogue,' Nana tutted. 'Anyway, back to the topic in hand. I am going to apply, and may the best woman win; although as neither of you want to be the angel, well, I reckon I stand a chance. Oh, and by the way, if you seriously think I'm too old, take a good look at all the Santas in grottos everywhere. Most of them are ancient – even older than me, if that's possible,' she said drily.

'Well,' said Shania, 'I think you'd make a fantastic angel, Nana Mary...'

'Cup of tea, Nana?' I interrupted. 'Shan, come and give me a hand,' I said, dragging her off the settee.

When we got into the kitchen out of Nana's ear range, I hissed at Shan. 'Don't be encouraging her. You know how much I love her, and I know you love her too, but really, do you want to spend six weeks being bossed around by Nana, as well as whoever else is there to boss us around? I can't say I'm thrilled with the prospect of the job, but I can see that it might actually be fun if me and you are both elves. And it would keep mam off me back.'

'Donna, Nana Mary is one of the funnest people I know. I think it would be great to work with her, so no can do. I'm not going to put her off, and nor should you.'

Every now and again I had to concede that

Shan was right, and this was one of those occasions. 'Oh, okay,' I said, somewhat chastened. 'But I tell you now, if I don't utter the words, "I told you so," at least a hundred times, then I'll show me backside in Renwick's window!'

We went back through with the tea and took our places at each side of Nana.

'Right, Shan,' I said. 'How do we apply for these jobs?'

'Just got to send an email. Oh, and a current "unfiltered" photo.' She burst into peals of laughter.

'Aye, that'll be right. I'm telling you, there'll be a support group for people addicted to filtering soon, if there isn't already; although they would all get a shock when they saw each other for the first time at the meetings.' Nana shook her head. 'In my day...'

'Er, what photo will we send for you, Nana?' I asked, wondering how she was going to cross this bridge unfiltered.

'Listen, pet, no such things as filters back in the day. I've got a lovely one of me from 1974 in the Blackpool Tower ballroom, as natural as the day I was born, legs like Red Rum.'

'Was he a ballet dancer, Nana Mary?' asked Shan.

'Nana, that makes the photo about fifty years old,' I said, counting on my fingers.

'Well, you can jazz it up a bit, can't you? Erm, not filter, just well, you know... a bit of titivation.'

'That is filtering, Nana, and I think they might notice when you get there.'

'Whatever do you mean?' she winked.

***

We were all sat in a row looking at our photo choices, cackling like the three witches in Macbeth, when my mam came in from work. Mam works in Go Your Own Way, the aforementioned funeral parlour where I lasted half a day as a trainee. It wasn't a complete disaster though; Mr Papadopoulos did get his space funeral idea out of me, and I never got a penny for that stroke of genius.

'What's all this?' Mam asked, eyeing us suspiciously. 'I don't like it when you three aren't all bickering with each other. It means you're up to something.'

She flopped into an armchair, kicked off her shoes and pulled down the zip of the hideous jumpsuit that Mr Papadopoulos insisted they wear as a uniform.

'Busy day, pet?' Nana asked. 'Donna, go and get your mam a cup of tea. And here, fill mine up,' she said, handing me her mug. 'Oh, and bring some biscuits.'

'Come on then, lighten my day up and tell me what you three are laughing at,' Mam said.

So, we told her!

# CHAPTER 3

'Mam, you must be kidding,' said my mam to Nana. 'You can't wear that dress; you'll look like the Bride of Chucky and scare the kids witless,'

'Eeh, don't be daft – they'll love me.'

'And what will everyone say?'

'I'm not bothered what anyone thinks. You don't care anymore when you get to my age,' said Nana, with the steely glint in her eye that told me she was now more determined than ever to become the Christmas Angel of the North. 'I'm doing this for women my age everywhere. You don't stop being an angel because you're a certain age. I mean look at the Angel Gabriel. How old is she?'

'He's a he... I think,' I said.

'Even better – everyone should be able to be an angel. Anyway, are you ready to send those applications, Shan? Press the button.'

'Gone,' Shan smiled. 'Hope we all get interviews.'

Mam shook her head, a resigned look on her face as she dunked her Hobnob into her tea.

\*\*\*

A few days later, Shan burst into the house screaming like a banshee.

'Donna, I got an interview for Renwick's. Have you?'

'I don't know. Haven't looked at my phone today – it's on charge.'

Shan looked at me as if I was an alien that had just descended. 'How can you let it run down? I'd be ready to take away if that happened to me. Go on quick, have a look!'

'You've got that nomophobia, you have.'

'What's that?' Shan asked, googling it immediately and proving my point by doing so.

I retrieved my phone and looked to see a little light flashing, indicating I had a new email. Sure enough, it was from Renwick's to say I too had been selected for interview. I quickly read the contents.

'Did you read all of it, Shan?'

'No. Too excited – just saw the first line and then ran here. Why, what does it say?'

'Tell you what; let's go to Nana's and see if she's heard, and then we can discuss it. But let's just say we are only over the first hurdle.'

Nana was in her kitchen, washing the dishes and listening to something that passed for music back in the day. It was an assault on the eardrums, something about an Irish fellow's goat, and even the cat hid when it came on.

'Alexa, shut the you-know-what up,' I yelled. 'NOW!'

'Donna, I was listening to that. Nearly at the best bit. What's up?'

'Did you get an email from Renwick's, Nana?'

'I don't know. My phone's on charge.'

Shan shook her head. 'I can see where you get it from now,' she sniggered.

'Go and get it, Donna pet. You'll have to sort it

for me anyway. Can't be doing with these smart-arse phones. All I want to do is ring someone and then hang up, like the old days. I used to love my slimline phone – such a lovely shade of orange.'

'Woo hoo!' I yelled, as I saw the email from Renwick's. It's a hat trick – we're all through.'

'Am I going to be the angel? I told you so...'

'Erm, not quite. Tell you what – I'll put the kettle on, then we can go through the emails and plan our next moves. Quite literally as it happens,' I said wryly.

Once we were all seated around Nana's tiny kitchen table, I went through the terms of our interviews.

'All the emails are the same. There's no mention of roles, just that they will select them based on who they feel will fulfil the brief best but...' I paused, 'what it does say is that we all have to prepare a short performance to showcase our talents in front of the Renwick's recruitment panel. It would appear that these jobs aren't just about cleaning up after kids but include keeping them happy with impromptu song and dance routines, magic tricks or whatever.'

Shan let out a big gasp, and I suddenly felt quite nauseous.

'What do you mean, performance? Like those kids in *Nativity* who have to audition and can't sing a note or fall off the stage?' asked Shan, looking far less confident than she had a few seconds ago.

'Aye, a bit like that, and all you can hear is the panel shouting, "Next!" I retorted. 'And even worse, they're being held in Renwick's social club, in front of an audience. First come, first served tickets it says here. We're doomed.'

Nana was the only one who didn't appear to be phased by such a challenge.

'Eeh, how exciting! I'm going to sing 'Paddy McGinty's Goat.' They'll love it, and I'll do a bit of tap dancing at the same time. It'll just be like that Michael Flarty fellow who did *Riverdance*. Here, I'll go put me shoes on and show you.'

'Er, that's okay, Nana. Why not keep it as a surprise until after you've practised?' I interjected before she went to get the tin tray to dance on – a party piece she never tired of but the rest of us had.

'Listen, I think I've got a plan,' said Shan. 'I could do keepie uppies and ball tricks while I mime to 'Fog on the Tyne.' It'll show them I'm fit enough to run around the grotto after kids all day, and even better, I can wear me Toon top.'

'You'll smash it, Shania,' said Nana, nodding in appreciation.

'As long as I don't smash the grotto lights,' she sniggered.

They then both turned their attention on me.

'And you, Donna? What are you going to do?'

# CHAPTER 4

A cold shiver shot down my spine. The very idea of performing anything in front of strangers filled me with dread.

'Oh, maybe I'm not cut out for the job after all. Besides, I'm busy writing a Christmas story for kids called *The Night Santa Got Lost in Lockley*,' I said, deflecting attention away from me having to do the audition.

Shan's mouth opened and closed like a dolphin popping up for air.

'Have you thought that story through, Donna? Doesn't sound like one of your better ideas. Does he pop in to see Beryl at Zoflora's for some of her special cookies, before heading to Tommy's for a Tattoo of Rudolph and coming out to find that Brad Balls and his scally mates have nicked the sleigh?' she laughed.

'Er, no, actually it's...' I began, only to be interrupted by Nana yelling.

'That's it! I've got it! You can do a *Jackanory* type presentation. Get dressed up as a Christmas cracker, or whatever, and read out your story. But Shania's right, Donna – I think maybe it might need a little work. Can he not get lost somewhere a bit posher, like that place all the footballers live? I expect they've got much bigger chimneys there, you know.'

'No, he cannot,' I grumbled. 'There's nothing wrong with getting lost in Lockley. Anyway, I'll have a think about the storytelling thing. We've got a few days to practise, so best get on with it. I'll just go and rewrite my entire story, eh, now you two have slated it, you pair of snobs!'

'Constructive criticism,' Nana smiled. 'Right, lasses, let's get our acts together. All for one and one for all, just like the Three Wise Women, except it won't be if I don't become the Christmas Angel of the North,' she winked, as she went off in search of her tap tray.

***

The day of our 'auditions' arrived, and I

was in danger of replicating Dolly Dixon's bowel problems, this being so far out of my comfort zone. On the other hand, Nana and Shan were beside themselves with excitement. We had arranged to meet at Nana's house in time to catch the 10.30 bus into town. Thing was, how on earth did I dare go outside looking more like Mrs Brown off the telly than I'd care to admit?

I had decided on dressing as Mrs Claus to read out my story, which, despite Nana's snobbery, was still called *The Night Santa got Lost in Lockley*. If I say so myself, it had bestseller written all over it, but perhaps that was my overenthusiasm with a Sharpie! I had raided the dressing up box at Lockley Library, aided by my friend and mentor, Miss Primm, lead volunteer, who had me looking like an octogenarian in the blink of an eye.

'I'll just tie this cushion around your middle, Donna, pad you out a bit, then you'll look the part,' she said, adjusting the curly grey wig she had popped on my head. 'Oh, and put these on.' She handed me a pair of small, round gilt spectacles.

'Oh my God, I can't see a thing in these,' I said, blinking. 'I'll never be able to read my story.'

Miss Primm took the glasses from my face and deftly pushed the lenses out of the frames.

'That better?' she enquired, as I looked at her through glassless glasses! She was very resourceful was Miss Primm, and one of my favourite people in the world – it was thanks to her patient coaching that I made the grade to get into university.

'Donna, I'm so very proud of you. All you need to do today is to be yourself. Read out your fabulous story with pride, and if they don't like it, they will have me to deal with,' she said, shaking her head until her two Princess Leia coiled plaits wobbled. 'Now off you go and meet the others for the bus.' She helped me into Dad's big topcoat, which covered most of my embarrassment.

I shoved the wig in my bag and waddled off down the road to Nana's, taking a short cut through the precinct. Big mistake! There was Brad Balls and his skanky mates outside Betty's Baps, no doubt working out what they could afford on last night's ill-gotten gains.

'Look lads, Mad Donna's up the duff! And I thought Madonna was a virgin,' Brad howled, laughing.

I was actually quite impressed with his wit. He was maybe not as dim as he looked.

'Coming from someone as thick as mince, Brad Balls, that was almost funny,' I rasped, trying to pick up speed in my Mrs Claus shoes, which were like a pair of Cullercoats Cobles on my feet.

I burst into Nana's, feeling about as Christmassy as an Advent Calendar in July.

'This had better be worth it,' I began, until I clocked Nana, who was dressed in so much green she resembled a cucumber. 'Nana!'

'What?'

'You look... er... well, green.'

'Aye, pet. That's because I'm a Christmas leprechaun. Shan got me the face paint at Pound Xpress. It's a nice shade, isn't it? Probably would be called *Green with Envy* on that paint chart thing.'

'More like *Chippie Tea Pea*,' I retorted. 'I hope it comes off. Remember when Shan turned blue like Papa Smurf, thanks to that cheap shell suit from there?'

'It'll be fine,' hissed Shan, who just looked

like she did every other day of the week in her Newcastle United top, shorts and trainers. Her one concession to Christmas was that she was wearing a Santa hat – a black and white one, naturally.

'Shall we get a taxi?' I asked, deciding that no matter what it cost, it would be worth not having to run the risk of yet another encounter with one of the Balls family. After all, there were plenty of them.

'A taxi?' shrieked Nana, like I'd suggested we hire a private jet. 'I've got me bus pass. Got to get me money's worth out of it at my age you know.'

'It was free,' I muttered.

Nana's cornflower blue eyes glinted at me through her mushy pea face.

'Okay, okay, you two,' interjected Shan, knowing where this could lead. 'I've got the casting vote, and we're going on the bus, so get your big knickers on, Mrs Claus, and stop being such a wuss.'

# CHAPTER 5

I think the short walk from the bus stop in town to Renwick's might go down as one of the worst experiences of my life. An ageing leprechaun, a waddling woman with boats on her feet and Lockley's answer to Alana Shearer doing keepie uppies as she walked along the crowded pavement, kind of drew attention. Geordies, whilst being the loveliest people on the earth, were also known for their cutting wit, and believe me, they were on form that morning.

'Look what you get when you order Atomic Kitten on Wish,' quipped one.

'The tide wouldn't take you lot out,' guffawed another.

'Halloween isn't until next week,' shouted the man selling fruit.

Then Shan was accosted by a woman pulling a

shopping trolley.

'Call yourself a carer. You should be ashamed! Taking more interest in that football than those poor old souls you're meant to be watching. She's green around the gills and doesn't look at all well,' she said pointing to Nana. 'You need to get her up the hospital quick smart.'

Shan shoved her football in her backpack, grabbed our arms, and dragged us towards Renwick's, with the woman still shouting abuse behind us. It seemed half of Northumberland Street were struggling to get their phones out to film the wicked carer neglecting her charges.

Once in the store, safely away from the throng, we made our way in the lift to the top floor and entered the Social Club. There we were met by Pandora Chumley-Smythe, Head of Social Activities, according to her shiny green and gold name badge.

Pandora wasn't the kind of girl we would have met at Lockley High. She oozed posh. The best word I could think of to describe her was wholesome. She was tall, her back ram rod straight and her glossy chestnut brown hair swept back in an immaculate chignon. Her well-fitted designer staff trouser suit was topped off with a neck scarf displaying horseshoes. Yep, Pandora looked the type that would have gone to pony club and had midnight feasts in the dorm of her boarding school, not chased scallies down the street to get her bike back. She nearly choked on her skinny yak milk chai latte, or whatever it was, when she saw us coming through the door.

'Oh, my word, you three look...' she struggled for words.

'Unique?' I offered.

'Hmm, well that sums it up, I suppose. I meant that no-one else has come in costume, so you rather stand out.'

'We're not in costume,' I said, keeping my face straight and staring into her perfectly made-up eyes. 'This is us every day of the week.'

'Oh, I see,' she faltered, before regaining her composure. 'So, we have Mary O'Keefe?'

'That's me, pet,' said Nana, curtsying like she was in the presence of royalty.

'Shania...Tw...Twine,' she read out, squinting

at her sheet and then looking at us questioningly.

'Here,' Shan replied, putting her hand up like she was back at school. 'And yes, I'm really called that thanks to me mam marrying that tool Richie Twine, otherwise known as Stringy Dick. Now long gone, thank gawd, but I'm stuck with the name,' she grimaced.

'At least she wasn't called after a bracelet,' I muttered.

'Erm, sorry I didn't catch that,' said Pandora. 'So, through a process of elimination you must be Donna Dobbs?'

'She's really called Mad Donna,' said Nana.

Pandora was beginning to look flushed in the face.

'Seriously? You are telling me we have Madonna and Shania here today?'

'Yes, pet, that's right.'

'I'm just plain old Donna now. I don't want to be the Mad bit anymore, so please just put Donna down on the form,' I grumbled.

'Erm, got it, I think. Now then follow me,' she said, after she had ticked our names off the list and ushered us into what she referred to as 'the green room.' It was already bustling with potential grotto recruits. I was sure this is what it would be like backstage at *Britain's Got Talent*. You couldn't breathe for Lynx Africa and hairspray.

'Make yourselves comfortable, and practise all you like. There are refreshments over there, so help yourselves. If you'll excuse me, as everyone is now here I need to address the room.'

'Address the flipping room,' I muttered. 'Shan, this is all your fault. I'm not sure if we're auditioning for a place in a shop grotto or the next production in the West End.'

Pandora teetered to the front of the room on her extremely high heels, picked up a glass and pinged it with a fork.

'If I can have your attention.' She attempted a smile, but I've seen a more genuine grin on a constipated cow. 'Thank you all for coming today. We had a lot of applications, and you are the chosen few, so well done for getting this far,' she gushed at us, like we had just been given an Oscar. 'Renwick's provides the best Christmas experience for children in the whole of the United Kingdom;

a bold statement, you may think, but we believe it to be true. We strive to find the best staff for our grotto. Renwick's has become something of a springboard for those in the entertainment field who often go on to stage and screen. In fact, our elf, Bobby, from last year is currently in discussions to join the cast of Geor...' She stopped abruptly, a look of pure distain crossing her face. 'Erm, a well-known reality show.' She continued hurriedly: 'And that is why most of you here today are from a theatrical background, but never let it be said that Renwick's ignores those from more, erm, diverse circumstances.'

I swear she looked in our direction as she said that.

'Smashing, Nana,' I hissed. 'We're the token randoms to tick their inclusivity box. But not to worry – you might get a part as a sausage roll in the next Greggs advert after this.'

'The process is that you will be called on stage to perform, the audience participating in the performance by holding up paddles...'

'Paddles?' enquired Nana. 'Are they going cruising up the Tyne or something? I did that and was seasick by the time we got to Wallsend.'

'Not quite, Mrs O'Keefe. These are paddles that our audience and judges hold up to identify if they are enjoying an act.'

'Just call me Mary, pet,' said Nana nodding.

'Er, okay, Mary. The paddles say "Hit" on one side and "Miss" on the other. If all paddles in the room show "Miss" you will hear a bell, and that is your audition over and you are free to leave. If you reach the end of your time without hearing the bell, please return to the green room and wait. Any questions?'

The room went as quiet as the night before Christmas.

'Well, as we say in the industry, good luck and break a leg, but hopefully not literally.' She cast a worried glance at me and Nana.

Once Pandora was out of earshot, I turned to Shan and Nana. 'I can't believe you dragged me here, Shan. The embarrassment. I might just bale out now. I mean, the three wild cards from Lockley who got the pity interviews against Newcastle's finest up-and-coming thespians – we're going to hear more bells than St Saviours, aren't we?'

'You're not going anywhere, Donna,' said Nana. 'You're an O'Keefe, and we don't bale – ever.'

Actually, I was a Dobbs, but now was not the time to challenge Nana's perception of the family tree, which in her view had stopped with her at O'Keefe.

'Trust me, you two. I've got this sorted,' said Nana, totally unconcerned, humming 'Paddy McGinty's Goat' while polishing her tray with her bright yellow duster. Nana looked too confident. She was up to something, that was for certain.

As Pandora made her way to the door, I clocked her giving a sly wink to a young woman who was mid-way through what looked like some sort of yoga exercise.

'Eeh, look at Bendy Wendy over there,' Nana cackled. 'I'm sure she was the contortionist on at Butlins last time I was there.'

'I bet that's Pandora's best mate,' I tutted. 'Seriously, is this what people go through just to be a flipping elf?' I turned to Shan whose unblinking eyes gazed around the room at the wannabe posing, tra-la-la-ing and taking selfies.

'Seems so,' she whispered back. 'Soz, Don mate

– we've got no chance, have we?'

'No, but Nana says we're stopping, so we might as well give it our best shot,' I said, the O'Keefe fighting spirit suddenly kicking in. 'At least they don't know what me and Nana look like, which is more than what can be said for you, so that's your penance for making us all look ridiculous. Still love you, though,' I grinned, and Shan threw her arms around me for a hug.

'How many months are you?' she guffawed, poking the cushion underneath my frilly Mrs Claus apron. 'You'll make a lovely mam one day, Donna Dobbs!'

# CHAPTER 6

Nana found her way to the refreshments table and made herself a cup of tea.

'Here, lasses – have you seen the buffet?' she said, as she came back to our seats. 'It's fabulous, and no one else seems to be interested.'

I understood why. Scoffing heather honey-coated pigs in blankets was probably not the best way forward before an audition.

'I'm pleased I brought me Tupperware box.'

'Nana! You can't. It's like stealing.'

'Listen, pet, it'll only go to waste, and it's for a good cause – I can make sure the poor old pensioners of Lockley benefit,' she laughed.

Shania straightened my wig, and I put the specs on.

'You need some rouge on those cheeks,' said

Nana, dipping into her bag and bringing out a little pink cardboard pot that looked like it might be from the 1960s. She circled some on my cheeks.

'Not like that, Nana Mary,' said Shan. 'TikTok says you sweep it lightly on the apples of the cheeks.'

'Mary Tok says you put it on so you can see it, otherwise what's the blinking point,' Nana replied, tongue out in concentration as she rubbed even harder.

I strolled over to the full-length mirror and wished I hadn't. I looked like a pantomime dame, never mind Mrs Claus. Just at that, the door to the green room opened.

'Watch out! Pandora the Explorer's back, and she's not alone,' said Shan, nodding towards the door.

I swear my heart missed a beat as I saw the most gorgeous guy I'd ever seen in actual real life come into the room. Mind you, that wasn't too difficult, as Lockley was hardly overrun with eligible men. I gulped, taking in his brooding magnificence, channelling my inner Elizabeth Bennet. He was tall and broad-shouldered with dark brown close-cropped hair. Even from this distance, I could see that his eyes were as bright green as Nana's face paint. He smiled to reveal beautiful, even teeth that clearly hadn't come from Turkey. He was wearing a white, fitted shirt which was tight across his muscular chest, a few open buttons revealing a smooth, golden tan. Dark tapered trousers gave enough of an idea that he enjoyed keeping fit, and his shoes looked very expensive. The executive style clothing gave him a look of Jamie Dornan in *Fifty Shades*, and I felt my insides turn to jelly, constricting in a warm band underneath my padding at the very thought of what it would be like with him in the boardroom (yes, I did say *boardroom!).* He wasn't my usual type. I'd never ever been out with anyone wearing a suit, let alone owning one; most of the lads in Lockley only ever borrowed them when they were making an appearance in court.

As he made his way over to the refreshment table, Pandora placed an arm territorially on his, guiding him. I hoped she wouldn't notice that quite a few of the plates were now prematurely empty. Pandora, however, was far too busy making goo-goo eyes at *my* Mr Grey Street to notice the absence of mini stollen, and I really didn't blame her – my heart still hadn't returned to its usual rhythm, and my eyes were transfixed on him.

'Sorry to interrupt,' she purred, 'but I want to introduce you all to a very important person. This is Nathaniel Renwick, son of Sir Oliver Renwick, our CEO.' I swear if she batted her eyelashes at him much more the overhead sprinklers would turn on. 'Nathaniel is our head judge today.'

Nathaniel had the grace to look embarrassed.

'Just call me Nate,' he laughed. 'And seriously, I'm really not that important.'

His voice was deep and far from the clipped tones I had expected. As Nana might say, he spoke the Queen's English, although to be factually correct I suppose it should be the King's English now. Nate's voice, however, held the slightest trace of a northern accent, which only served to make him even more blooming gorgeous! Pandora took Nate around the room, introducing him to the auditionees, who licked up to him like he was Lord Webber. I thought Bendy Wendy was going to combust her chakras. When they had circled the room, Pandora grabbed Nate's arm and made a beeline for the door – without bringing him to the corner where we were.

'Here, pet, haven't you forgotten about us?' Nana shouted, not one to ever miss out.

'Erm, sorry Mrs er Mary. We're on a tight schedule,' said Pandora.

But Nate was having none of it. He came over, took Nana's hand and gave it a shake.

'Lovely to meet you, Mary, is it? You make a fabulous Christmas leprechaun! Are you Irish, by chance?'

'No, pet, Newcastle born and bred. But I was married to Donal O'Keefe – as Irish as St Paddy himself, but he was no saint let me tell you…'

'Er, maybe another time,' interrupted Pandora. 'Nathaniel, this is Madonna and Shania who are here with Mary today.' She flicked on a disingenuous smile, which could have easily been mistaken for wind.

I could see Nate's gorgeous green eyes beginning to crinkle at the corners at the mention of our names, but clearly the gentleman, he managed to rein in his mirth.

'Just Donna,' I glowered at Pandora.

'Oh, yes, sorry. *Donna*, Mary and Shania aren't perhaps our typical candidates, but we couldn't bypass their applications as all have, erm, performed in the past. As you know, Renwick's strives to be inclusive. Mary and Donna, I want you to know that we here at Renwick's are proud of our diversity policy. Everyone is treated on their ability to do the job and well, erm, other factors don't really matter, do they Nathaniel?'

I was just about to say, 'Like age you mean,' but then stopped mid thought. The penny had just dropped and rolled directly into my subconscious, like the big star counter in *Tipping Point*. They thought I was the same age as Nana. Oh my God, I wished the floor would part and drop me down to the Menswear Department directly underneath us.

'Absolutely not,' Nate nodded, grabbing my hand and shaking it. His green eyes looked directly into mine through the metal rims of my spectacles. If there had been any glass in them, they would have been totally steamed up – I felt like I might literally melt with desire, and it was a struggle to drag my eyes away from his. 'And is it appropriate for me to say Mrs, er, Mad, I mean

Donna, that we can provide you with a seat if your legs get too tired. I notice you are wearing special shoes.' He gazed at the large, ugly footwear I was sporting.

'Erm, thanks,' I squeaked, not quite knowing what else to say. My entire face must now be the colour of my rouged cheeks – I probably looked like Snow White's shiny red apple. Before he turned to Shan, I couldn't help a last sneaky look at his beautiful green eyes, which up close were like a kaleidoscope pattern. Tiny swirls of glossy rich holly mingled with highlights of bright green mistletoe. His proximity to me also revealed he smelled divine, his scent a perfect match for those beautiful citrusy eyes. He had a very enthusiastic conversation about football with Shan and looked so much more relaxed than he had done when he entered the room. Pity the same couldn't be said about Pandora, who looked as tense as a violin string as she tried to hurriedly steer him towards the door.

# CHAPTER 7

'He's nice, isn't he?' said Shan, once we were alone.

'He is,' I replied non-committally, hoping she didn't notice my flushed face; though that was futile, as Shan could always read me like the book I wanted to write.

'You like him, don't you?' she squealed.

'Keep your voice down,' I hissed.

'I'd fancy him myself, if he was my type,' she howled. 'He smelled good enough to eat. I bet he can just help himself to anything in the store. Imagine that. I'd be straight to Sports to get those trainers I'll never afford.'

'I doubt he can just take anything, Shan, but he probably gets all kinds of freebie samples. I'd be circling that Beauty Hall like Jaws.'

'Do you think he's single and ready to jingle,

Don?'

'Well, even if he is, which I doubt, as it looks like Pandora might have her claws into him, he's not going to fall for someone old enough to be his granny is he?'

'What, like Nana, you mean?'

'No, like me. Shan, have you noticed what I look like at the moment?'

Shan looked me up and down.

'Aye, you've got a point. You're not looking your best. Never mind, mate – there's always Brad Balls if you can't have Brad Pitt!'

The auditionees were ready to take to the stage. The first, a big lad in a massive Christmas jumper, was going to sing 'Nessun Dorma.' Or attempt to. I couldn't help but wonder how that might be a useful talent for working as an elf.

The door swung open, and Big Lad jumped to attention thinking he was on. I couldn't believe my eyes when I saw Miss Primm come into the room accompanied by six of The Lockley Cheeky Chicks Reading Club. She spotted us in the corner and shepherded her charges towards us. They looked adorable, all dressed as tiny elves, and I could see that the Knit and Natter group must have had a hand in making the costumes. Little Babatunde's had a few extra frills, and I could almost guarantee Old Joe made it!

'What's all this?' I asked, as twelve full moon eyes blinked up at me.

'These are your supporting actors, Donna,' Miss Primm smiled. 'Now children, remember what we discussed. You must be on your best behaviour; do what we practised and listen to Donna.' And at that she turned on her heel and left.

'You talk like Mad Donna, but you don't look like her, innit,' accused Boris Balls, mini Geordie gangster, aged four, going on fourteen.

'It is her,' said his twin, Bambi. 'You can tell by her makeup; she always looks like that.' She then poked me in the leg and pulled on my skirt until I was down to her level when she whispered in my ear. She rocked back to look at me, enormous periwinkle blue eyes twinkling in a heart shaped face, her pink rosebud lips pursed in anticipation. Bambi Balls was a doll, cute as a button, a picture of innocence… until she opened her mouth.

'Miss Primm said you would give us money *if* we behave. I want to buy a Bluey. A real one that talks. Not a pretendy one from Pound 'Spress that sounds funny.'

The blue eyes narrowed. I was being extorted by a four-year-old!

'I am sure Miss Primm didn't say that. How about some cake instead?' I pointed towards the now depleted refreshment table.

'Ten pounds each,' she shouted as she shot off to join five other pairs of robust little legs in stripey tights, dashing towards what was left of the sweet treats.

'Did you know about this, Nana?' I demanded.

'Listen, pet, there's nothing wrong with being inventive is there? Just get them to sit in a circle – they know what to do...'

As if I didn't have enough to worry about.

Big Lad went through the doors of shame. We weren't allowed to watch, so we all gathered to try and listen for the sound of the reject bell. If it had rung, we wouldn't have heard and nor would Big Lad, because he could belt them out louder than

Michael Ball at the Last Night of the Proms. As he reached the crescendo of the song, I swear the floor began to shake, although that might have been down to the elves, high on sugar, running around the room like they were at Jumpin' Jack's Play Barn.

Big Lad's face was the same colour as mine as he burst back through the door, high on adrenaline.

'No bells for me,' he said smugly. 'I think it's in the bag!'

'Were you mainly hit or miss?' I asked, curious as to whether there was some kind of system going on.

'None of your business, Mrs Doubtfire,' he said testily.

'Mrs Claus to you,' I retorted, guessing from his response that he had more misses than hits.

The next few contestants went on, and not one person got bonged off. I reckoned Renwick's didn't want to destroy anyone's confidence. Bendy Wendy pirouetted to the door like she was about to take the stage in *Swan Lake*.

'Good Luck,' Nana shouted to her retreating

back. 'I enjoyed you at Butlins.'

'Butlins? Her?' said a serious-faced girl, leaning against the wall, waiting for her turn and looking totally bored. 'She won't even know what Butlins is, and she won't need good luck. That's Persephone, Pandora's best mate. She used to be in my drama class until Daddy paid for her to go to some swanky academy in London.'

'Per what?' asked Nana and Shan in unison.

'I need to see this,' I whispered. 'I'm sneaking out to watch. Keep an eye on the kids Nana – they were your idea after all.'

I snuck into the social club and stood at the rear, surveying the backs of the heads of the audience. There was a small stage, and in front of that was a long table with four people sat in a row: the official judges. I could see Mr Grey Street's side profile as he chatted to the man next to him, and I was catapulted into another dimension where me and Nate were skiing down a snow-covered mountain in Switzerland in perfect tandem. I'd never even seen a ski before, let alone been to Switzerland – maybe I'd been watching too much *Emily in Paris*. But before I could get as far as the apres-ski activity, my delicious daydream was cut short; I heard a familiar voice drift from the front which brought me down to earth quicker than a tumble on a black ski run.

'She's going to be singing and dancing to "Let it Go" from *Frozen*. That's one of me favourites.'

And at that the voice burst into song.

'Lerrit go...lerrit go...' it warbled.

'You'd better let it go, Joe, or else I'll be stitching your mouth up,' said the less than dulcet tones of none other than Dolly Dixon.

'Pity you can't stitch your backside up, Dolly,' retorted Joe, cut off in his prime.

'Ssh, you two. She's coming on.'

The voice of Miss Primm floated down the small auditorium, and it was then I realised that the whole of the front row was taken up by members of Lockley Knit and Natter Group. No wonder Nana had looked so confident.

The spotlight fell on Persephone, and she floated around the stage wearing a beautiful ice blue dress, her long blonde hair in a fishtail plait. I had to concede she looked lovely, and her voice wasn't too shabby either. The auditorium filled with cheers and applause at the end as the paddles began to go up. I could see the reverse sides of the boards facing me and could tell that Persephone had got nearly a full house of Hits – apart from the front row, where all, except for Joe, must be displaying a Miss. I spotted Dolly grabbing Joe's paddle and swinging it around out of his reach, much to his annoyance.

I made my way back to the green room.

'Nana! How could you. It's cheating,' I hissed.

'What's cheating?' Shan asked.

'Ask her.' I pointed my finger at Nana.

'Miss Primm said I was cheating when I went up the snake in Snakes and Ladders,' said Bambi Balls. 'Cheating is for losers.' Bambi made the L sign with her chubby little fingers and held it to her forehead.

'Pity Miss Primm doesn't lead by example,' I muttered. 'I'm shocked. How did you persuade her to do it, Nana?'

'Donna, she's doing it for you. After me and your mam and dad, Lavinia Primm is your biggest supporter and, well, we all felt that doing something out of your comfort zone would be a brilliant opportunity to prepare you for meeting strangers when you get to university. Lavinia is doing this out of love, and she felt it was worth swallowing her principles for. Let's face it, you've made a ham's fist of every other job you've tried so far, so it was worth a go. I'll even let you be the Christmas Angel of the North if you want, my pet. I'd give you my last, you know that don't you?'

What could I say to that? Nothing, as I was too choked to respond, so I gave Nana a big hug and got green paint all over my snowy Mrs Claus pinny for my troubles!

# CHAPTER 8

'Right,' said Nana, changing the subject. 'You're up next, Shan. Off you go and kick their backsides.'

We listened at the door as the familiar beat to 'Fog on the Tyne' began. The audience, or maybe it was just the stool pigeons in the front row, were obviously participating as there were cheers and clapping, and the odd 'Toon Army' chant. As the song ended, the clapping and shouting for more was deafening. Nana gave me a sly wink.

'They didn't do that for me,' Big Lad sniffed, shaking his head and looking despondent.

'Or me,' said Persephone, while still beaming with confidence.

Shan jumped back through the door, dribbling her football.

'Donna man, that was amazeballs! I loved it, and the audience seemed to like it. Even them ones in the front row, and they look like a right hard lot to please,' she winked.

Serious Girl was up next, returning looking even more bored than before, if that were possible. And then all too quickly it was my turn.

'I need a drink,' I said, feeling like I was about to head to the gallows.

'No, you don't, Donna,' tutted Nana, who only ever had a drink on high days and holidays whatever they were. 'All you need to do is be your canny little self, pet.'

'Nana Mary's right, Don – you only need to let your inner light shine through. I can see it now hovering above your head. It's a bit dull, mind.'

I gawped at Shan.

'What are you talking about?'

'Beryl Balls says you have to Love your Light. It's her new thing. I was her guinea pig and I'm telling you; your light needs some attention.'

'Shan, everything that woman does is a scam. She'll have just trawled the internet looking for her next way to earn a few quid.'

'Chillax man, Donna, and let your inner light

shine through. I'll book you a session.'

'Have you been eating her special cookies by any chance?'

'How very dare you. My body is a temple to sport, but I might have had a sample of her new range when I was there – all in the name of research you understand – they're called Canni Biskits. Bet even you couldn't have come up with that one!'

'And very canny they are too. I highly recommend them – great for achy joints,' said Nana. 'Anyway, back to business – line up behind Mrs Claus, Cheeky Chicks.'

'That's Mad Donna not Mrs Claus, innit,' giggled Boris.

'She's Mrs Claus today. Now then, just remember what we practised. If you are good, Miss Primm and the volunteers will take you to the Toy Department afterwards.'

They were the magic words. The six lined up like new recruits in a military parade. Nana went along the row as if she was the sergeant major inspecting the troops, wiping the evidence of their assault on the buffet off their faces with a napkin.

And we were good to go.

I shuffled onto the stage, followed by my little brood of elf chicks. A chair had been placed in the middle, and as I glanced at Mr Grey Street on the judges table, he pointed to it, gave me the thumbs up, then smiled a smile that would have lit up the Christmas tree in the Central Station. Nate had the power to literally knock me off my feet. I slumped into the chair, letting out a contented 'ahh' like I heard Nana do every time she sat down. The children sat cross legged on the floor in a semi-circle like perfect little angels, although I'm sure Bambi now had pound signs in her eyes. They watched me intently as I opened the cover of the big Christmas book I'd made myself to use as a prop. It had the Renwick's logo emblazoned on the back. Maybe there was more of Nana in me than I'd like to admit. Putting on my best Mrs Claus voice, assuming Mrs Claus was a Geordie that is, I began to read.

'*The Night Santa got lost in Lockley*, a story by Donna Dobbs, read by me, Mrs Claus.

"*It was Christmas Eve and Santa Claus was steering his sleigh high above the sleeping city of Newcastle. He looked down at the many bridges crossing the wide river and smiled. Not too much further and he would be out to sea where he would follow the coastline to his next destination, the tiny Holy Island of Lindisfarne. Santa's ancient weather watcher, a hawk called Egbert the One Eyed, was tucked away in the front of the sleigh and had decided to have a sneaky snooze on his perch. Egbert missed the changes in the atmosphere which should have prompted him to alert Santa that the Fog on the Tyne was about to swirl. And swirl it did, leaving Santa hopelessly lost in a thick mizzle..."'*

The more I read, the more my confidence increased and very soon the children were right there on that sleigh with Santa, and even the adult audience seemed to be listening to every word. Nate was hooting and booing appropriately throughout. Pandora, however, seemed bemused by the whole thing. I'm not sure she would have understood the nuances of life in Lockley. I thought the entire Knit and Natter club might be ejected from the auditorium for their over enthusiastic participation. It was magical for me to think my words were being so enjoyed and had the power to activate the imaginations of young (and old) minds. As I said, 'The End,' I felt sure that one day there was a chance of me realising my dream to write a book, if I managed to stick at it.

I had no idea what my paddle boards said as I floated back through to the green room, but I didn't care – I was on a high. I scooped Bambi Balls up and gave her a hug.

'I'll make sure you get your Bluey. I'll have a chat with Santa next time we speak to each other.'

'A proper Bluey?'

'Yes, a proper one.'

'Thank you, Mrs Donna Claus,' Bambi smiled sweetly. 'And maybe you can tell him that our Boris would like a snake – a great big real one with a long tongue!'

# CHAPTER 9

Nana was the final act.

'Good luck, Nana. Go and show them how to entertain people,' I shouted.

'Whoop whoop! You've got this, Nana Mary,' Shan smiled.

Nana gave her large tray a final polish and disappeared through the double doors.

'Stuff this,' I said, 'I'm going to watch her. I don't care what they say – it's her starring moment and I'm not going to miss it.'

'Try stopping me from seeing her too,' grinned Shan.

'And us,' said Bambi, as six little elves formed a crocodile behind us.

'I've got FOMO,' announced Big Lad, like he had the flu or something. 'It's a real condition you know, and I'm not cured yet. My counsellor said it might take a while, so I'm coming too. Anyone else in?' He gazed around the room.

It would appear everyone had caught FOMO from Big Lad, and the whole of the green room emptied as we made our way to the back of the auditorium to witness Mary O'Keefe, First Lady of Lockley, strut her stuff in her quest to become the Christmas Angel of the North.

As the opening bars of 'Paddy McGinty's Goat' began and Nana started to sing, it was absolutely apparent she was in her happy place. Even I could see that she was born to be on the stage. She had the audience captivated from the start, and really didn't need her fan club in the front row, who were on their feet within seconds and joining in. Nana was hilarious, moving around the stage, mimicking milking a goat and acting out the song lyrics. When the music changed to the tin penny whistle and percussion score of *Riverdance*, Nana placed her tin tray down and began to tap until I swear sparks were coming off it! Everyone in the audience was on their feet cheering her on, except Dolly Dixon who thankfully stayed seated, leaving nothing to chance.

I saw Nana gesture to the man operating the music to cut. Everything went quiet.

'Oi needs a nice young man to dance wit me,' shouted Nana down the microphone, in an odd hybrid accent, like a cross between her and Granda Dolan. I could see her surveying the front of the auditorium looking for a willing victim. Her eyes alighted on the judge's table, and she pointed directly at Mr Grey Street. 'You, young Nate me lad – come on get yourself up here. It's you or Old Joe, and he's got two left feet.'

'I have not,' shouted Joe good naturedly, 'but me hips aren't up to that malarkey anymore, so go on, my son, or we won't hear the end of it.'

Oh my God, Nana was asking Nathaniel Renwick to go and do Irish dancing on a tin tray with her. I looked at the back of Pandora's head and it was swinging from side to side like a pendulum as she tried to grab Nate's arm. But Nate didn't hesitate. He leapt out of his chair and onto the stage like he was Michael Flatley himself.

'I'd be delighted to join you, Mrs Mary. You just show me what to do.'

Nate then began a very entertaining warm

up routine, by which point my body was doing a warmup of an entirely different kind! Gyrating his very flexible hips, like a cross between Patrick Swayze and Magic Mike, he rolled up his sleeves to reveal muscular forearms covered in fine dark hair and a jumble of bands on his wrist. He then undid a few more buttons on his shirt, and by then it wasn't just me who was hyperventilating. I was really concerned for Old Joe, who looked like he could combust into confetti!

As the music struck up again, Nana took Nate by the hand (lucky her) and slowly began to tap. Nate followed her steps, and what he lacked in experience he more than made up for in enthusiasm. Within seconds, the room was buzzing. Nate Renwick was not the slightest bit phased by the potential of making a fool of himself. Not that he ever could – well not in my eyes, that is. Shan had been tapping along from the off and suddenly ran towards the stage.

'You look after the kids,' she shouted over her shoulder. 'You can't dance in those stupid shoes. I'm going to join in. I'm not missing out on this.'

She ran down to the front, leapt onto the stage, took Nate's other hand and the three of them began to jig in tandem. Pandora was on her feet in an instant and followed Shan onto the stage. The disgruntled look on her face was priceless! She kicked off her shoes, shoved Shan aside and grabbed Nate's hand. She had the grace of a carthorse, which only added to the humour.

Little Bambi Balls had eyes the size of Shan's football as she watched Pandora continue to keep pushing Shan out of the way. Bambi adored Shan, and there was a code of looking after your own in Lockley, which even at the grand old age of four, Bambi and twin Boris had learned. Gathering her troops, Bambi and her army of elves belted towards the stage and climbed on. I stood rooted to the spot hoping they were going to behave. They surrounded Pandora and forced her to move away from Nate and dance with them instead. Pandora tried to get out of the circle they had formed around her, but these little elves weren't going to be defeated. Shan bounced her way back, reclaimed her place and danced with Nana and Nate for the final few bars of the song.

'More! More!' shouted the audience as the trio took a bow. Nate was laughing, his face beaming with happiness, and he gave both Nana and Shan a hug. Pandora, waiting for her turn, looked furious when Nate totally ignored her and crouched down amongst the elves, giving a round of high fives.

The show was over, and the audience began to depart. Miss Primm gathered the kids to take them for their well-deserved visit to the Toy Department, and we made our way back to the green room to await our fate.

'Eeh, get me a cuppa, Donna pet. Me name's Herbert, and I'm parched.'

'Who's Herbert, Nana Mary?' Shan asked.

'Not a clue, pet, but me mam used to say it.'

'Well deserved cuppa coming up, Nana. You were brilliant.'

'I loved every minute. Listen you two, I know I'm not going to get the job, but it was worth coming just to get back on a stage again. It's been a long time.' Nana grinned.

'You deserve the job,' I said, handing her a cup of tea and the one remaining boring fig roll that was left.

'We all deserve the jobs,' said Nana. 'Here, I might as well eat an Odour Eater as this fig roll. Be a pet and get me one of Beryl's Canni Biskits out of me Tupperware box – guaranteed to perk me back up!'

# CHAPTER 10

We sat waiting for what felt like ages. Big Lad said his audition nerves were playing up and he was back and forwards to the loo, but we all knew he was earwigging at the door.

'Pandora and Nathaniel are having a very heated discussion,' he said theatrically, rubbing his hands together in glee. 'Couldn't quite hear what they were saying though. Maybe they are debating having me as the very first male Christmas Angel of the North.'

'You'll never fit in that frock, pet,' said Nana, sipping her tea.

'Nana, you can't say things like that anymore,' I whispered.

'Oh, here we go. Why not? It's true, isn't it? He'll look like a burst couch in that frock,' she hissed back at me.

'Er, hello! So would you, Grandma,' he retaliated. 'You're like about a hundred years old. No right to be here taking chances away from us young professionals.'

'Hoy, Mr Go Compare or whoever the heck you are, you can't say things like that anymore – it's ageist. And by the way, I am a proper professional.'

'Pot calling kettle, Nana,' I laughed.

'Any more quips like that,' Shan growled, 'and I'll be adding a couple of what are probably very tiny balls to my collection. Do you understand, Pavagrotti? Just shut the—'

Thankfully the door opened just at the right moment and in came Pandora and Nate, who were met with a wall of silence.

'Are you all rendered speechless through anticipation?' asked Pandora through gritted teeth. Her face was flushed, and her eyes were glassy with tears that she was struggling to hold back.

'Do *you* want to tell them, Mr Renwick?' she said pointedly at Nate.

'No, Pan, I'll leave that to you.'

Pandora coughed, clearing her croaky voice.

'Firstly, thank you all for coming today. As usual, the standard was extremely high. This year we had somewhat more, erm, variety than usual, which made our decision making even more difficult.'

I could tell Pandora was choosing her words very carefully.

'I am sure that those of you in the theatrical world will go on to great things in the future. If it's a no from us today, then don't despair and do try again next year, because, unfortunately, we only have limited vacancies. So, without further ado, the first role of elf goes to…'

'Drum roll, please,' smiled Nate.

'Shania Twine,' said Pandora, almost spitting the words out.

A gasp went around the auditionees, and all eyes turned to Shan.

'That don't impress me much,' said Big Lad.

'If you knew how many times I've heard that line.' Shan shook her head. 'You could at least try to be original or say what you actually think, if you're brave enough because believe me, you'd only say it once.'

'Congratulations, bestie!' I threw my arms around Shan. Nana joined in, and we had a group hug.

'You really deserve it, Shania,' said Nana.

'She does,' Nate nodded.

Pandora's mouth was now such a tight thin line, it looked like it had been drawn on with a biro, and we could hardly make out what she was saying.

'The next and final role of elf goes to...' she stopped, like she could hardly bear to say the words.

'Mrs Mary O'Keefe!' Nate yelled, rushing towards Nana, picking her up and twirling her around.

'Mary, you will be an asset – not just to the grotto but to the whole store. Congratulations, and welcome to the Renwick's family.'

Me and Shan screamed out in joy.

Nana, whilst smiling, didn't look overly happy.'

'An elf you say? she asked.

'Yes, Mrs O'Keefe, an elf.' Pandora had regained the power of speech. 'Don't tell me you thought you might be the Christmas Angel of the North?'

'And why shouldn't she be?' I said defensively.

'Well for one thing—'

'The only reason,' said Nate, cutting Pandora off, 'is that Mary is far too entertaining to be the Christmas Angel of the North, which is much more of a sedate role, suited to someone far less entertaining. Mary's bubbly personality suits the role of elf perfectly.'

Pandora looked ready to explode.

'Oh, I see,' said Nana. 'Well in that case, I'm delighted to be an elf.'

'Which brings us on to the *main* role of the day,' said Pandora with a heavy emphasis on the word main. Whilst Nate may assume The Christmas Angel of the North is a sedate role, it is far from that. The role of the angel goes back almost to the beginning of Renwick's Department Store and holds a special place in our history. The angel participates in many of our promotional activities across the store during festive season; therefore, for this incredibly special role we needed someone multi-faceted who can mix with our most valued customers. There really was only one person for the job, and I am delighted to announce that this year's Christmas Angel of the North will be… drum roll Nate, seeing as you're so good at them… Persephone Tompkinson-Todd.'

'Fix,' muttered bored girl, grabbing her bag and making a beeline for the door.

'Congratulations, Percy,' said a very unenthusiastic Nate to a beaming Persephone, who twirled around the room like she was Anton du Beke.

'You were the obvious choice, Percy,' said Pandora.

'Oh, Donna pet, this isn't right. You haven't been chosen. We can't do this without you – all for one and one for all, remember. I'm quitting in solidarity with you. Shania needs the money, so she should still take the job.'

'No way, Nana Mary. I'm quitting too. We came together, and we'll go together. I'm not staying without you two.'

'Honestly, it's okay. You and Shan will have such a good time, and maybe I'm not really entertaining enough for this kind of work. Anyway, let's pack up and get back to Lockley.'

Nate rattled on Nana's tin tray, which was propped up against the wall, nearly deafening us in the process.

'What's all this about quitting? We're not quite finished yet. We were all so impressed with Donna's story and the way she captivated all of us, that I spoke to my father after the auditions, and he agreed that we could create a new and very special role in this year's grotto. Mrs Claus will be Santa's right-hand woman, and she will also present story sessions across the day. How does this sound, Mrs Claus? Will you have enough stories to share?'

'Yes, she will,' Shan yelled, replying for me. She dived towards Nate and gave him a fist bump. 'We're Lockley lasses Nate – you can rely on us!'

# CHAPTER 11

Nana squeezed my arm then went off towards our corner. I followed her over.

'Are you okay, Nana?' I turned her around to see big tears rolling down her green cheeks, leaving wide track marks, like someone had mowed the first strip of lawn.

'Eeh, pet, he was right you know,' she sniffed.

'Who was?'

'That Big Lad. I've had my time, Donna; I shouldn't be taking opportunities away from you young people. My days touring with the Troupe Romano were some of the best of my life. It's how I met your Granda Dolan when we were performing in Derry.'

So not that great, I smiled to myself. Soon after meeting Granda, Nana had returned to Lockley, and the minute they were married she hung up her tap shoes. She started working at the pickle factory the very next day, but that's a whole other story.

'Nana! That is absolute nonsense. And you're being ageist – to yourself. You outshone every one of us up on that stage today and rightfully earned your place. If Big Lad actually had a personality to go with his voice, then he would have got the job, but he hasn't. So can you stop this now, please, because we are going to have the best time.' Even I had started to believe this now.

'You're not sad that you're not the angel, are you?' I asked, giving her a hug.

'No, pet, not sad at all. I'm more cut out to be an elf and entertain the kids. At least Big Lad didn't get to squeeze his bulky backside into that beautiful frock, so every cloud...'

When Shan came back, we gathered our stuff and headed into the foyer to make our way down to the ground floor. Pandora, Persephone and Nate were having an altercation right in front of the lift. They didn't see us coming out of the green room, so we stayed at a distance and listened in.

'So, not only do I have to work with those three very common down and outs – two pensioners and a football hooligan no less,' whined Persephone, 'but then you announce that Santa's helper is to be Mrs Claus and not the Christmas Angel of the North, who has always been in overall charge of the grotto. Just what is it that you expect me to do?'

'Just do what you do best, Percy. Float around in a designer ballgown doing nothing and continue to be the absolute snob that you are.' And at that Nate strode off down the corridor.

I thought I might love Nate Renwick!

Pandora and Persephone watched him go, their mouths flapping like baby chicks waiting for worms.

'What on earth's got into him?' wailed Pandora.

'Oh, you know Nate. He's always on the side of the underdog, and he's got a whole pack of cross breeds to champion this time,' Persephone smirked.

They both burst into peals of laughter, and I had to physically hold Shan back. Nana just stood stock still, taking it all in, which was more worrying, as I knew how conniving she could be.

'He's never going to take me to the Renwick's Ball now, though, is he? sniffed Pandora. I have dreamt about that all year. I've already got my gown, and now it's probably never going to happen. It's all right for you, Percy. You're engaged to Tristan.'

Shan snorted at the mention of the name, and I poked her in the ribs while trying not to laugh myself.

'Oh my God,' I whispered. 'Persephone and Tristan. Sounds like one of those Shakespeare tragedies Miss Primm made me read.'

'And we thought our mams were nuts choosing our names,' Shan laughed.

'Anyway, Pandora,' Persephone continued, 'it's not all over until the fat lady sings, and that fat Mrs Donna woman looks like she couldn't throw a Brussels sprout, never mind a tune. Did you see those hideous shoes she was trying to walk in?' They burst into cackles of laughter yet again.

'At least he's not going to be interested in any of them. Suppose that's one less thing to worry about,' Pandora barked.

The lift arrived, and the Ugly Sisters got in. I

hoped it would take them straight down into the basement of Hell where they truly belonged.

# CHAPTER 12

When we got back to the house, Orange Morgan, my brother's very pregnant girlfriend, was beached on the settee like a giant pumpkin; although in fairness, since Mam banned her from going to Stand By Your Tan while she's pregnant, she's now faded to butternut squash yellow.

'Oh my God, look at the state of you three, and you've got the cheek to call *me* names,' she cackled, while sticking one of her four-inch false eyelashes back in place. I'm surprised she could see anything out of what looked like two baby blackbirds roosting on her face.

'Have you got nothing better to do, like go and give birth to a baby tangerine, because you do know it's going to come out pre-tanned, don't you?'

'Oh, just shut your face, Mrs Bucket.'

'Well?' asked Mam, coming into the room. 'Are we celebrating or commiserating?'

'Like there was any doubt,' Nana smiled. 'We all got jobs. Start our training on Monday.'

'And who got to be the Christmas Angel of the North?' she asked.

'None of us,' said a very disgruntled Nana.

'Don't tell me you're surprised,' said Morgan, a look of pure joy on her face at our rejection. 'They'd have to have been desperate to choose one of you three. Maybe I'll apply next year.'

'Aye, do that Morgan. You're about the same colour as the Angel of the North. It'll be a shoe-in.'

'It was a fix; some friend of the boss got the job,' Nana continued. 'They obviously saw I had more talent than just being decorative, which is all that Perspexy lassie, or whatever the heck she's called, is good for. She might as well just be sitting on the top of the Christmas tree. I'd like to shove her arse on that spikey top branch myself.'

'Mother!' said my mam.

Shan and I struggled to keep our faces straight.

'It all worked out well in the end though, Mam,'

I said. 'It's a job, which is what you wanted. I'll be out of your hair and away from our squatter over there. I am now Mrs Claus, and I tell you for nowt, Morgan, you are not on this year's nice list!'

\*\*\*

Monday came around all too quickly, and once again we were top floor bound in Renwick's lift, for our training day. Only I went in costume. I quite liked hiding behind my Mrs Claus persona. Nana and Shan had opted for their usual clothes, which actually meant that Shan looked practically the same as she had on audition day. We entered the green room, where a handful of staff greeted us.

'Welcome, welcome,' said an older man.

'Norman!' Shan yelled, rushing across the room to give him a hug. 'What are you doing here?'

'I'm Santa Claus. I've been here at Renwick's for years. B&Q let me off over Christmas, and it's great to get away from plumbing for a few weeks. It's a right honour as it goes, listening to the dreams of the bairns.'

I could see Nana looking intently at him.

'That's Norman? I thought she said he was

about ninety-six. He looks more or less the same age as me I reckon, the cheeky young mare.' Nana whispered.

'Norman, this is Donna. She's going to be your wife; I mean your grotto wife, this year,' said Shania.

'Aye, I heard I was getting a new assistant. Pleased to meet you, Donna love. I hear you are a writer.'

If I wasn't already puffed up in my padding, I think I might have swelled to bursting point with pride.

'Erm, one day maybe. So nice to meet you.' Norman was as canny as Shan said he was.

'And who might this be?' Norman's eyes twinkled, looking at Nana.

'Mary O'Keefe at your service, Santa,' said Nana, and I'm sure her *Seductive Pink* cheeks deepened even further.

The door burst open and in came Big Lad from the auditions.

'Tah Dah! Greetings, Grotties. Not met most of you, but I bet some of you are surprised to see me again.' He scanned the room until he spotted us. 'An elf dropped out at the last minute, so here I am,' he grinned, jazz hands all aquiver.

He came across to where we were standing.

'Listen, we didn't get off to a great start at the auditions. My nerves get the better of me in those situations, and my inner diva takes over to get me through. I call her Mae West, and she can be cutting! I'm sorry for what she said. Can we start again, pretty pleeese? All newbies together? I'm Barry most days; Mae when I'm hangry!'

'Well, Bazza lad, we'll try to keep you well fed,' said Norman. 'Welcome aboard.'

So Bazza Big Lad wasn't so bad after all, which was more than can be said for the next person that marched in through the door.

Pandora.

'Ey up,' Norman smiled. 'Stand by your beds – ice queen incoming.'

'Welcome, Renwick's Christmas grotto team. Those of you who have been with us before know the drill, but for the benefit of our new staff, I'll go through a few things.' Pandora got straight down to business.

'First of all, it's the exciting announcement of what this year's theme is, and I think it is the best we have ever come up with. The grotto this year is to be Renwick's Mini Magical Shopping Land, consisting of a shopping village for children, with various mini play departments filled with age-appropriate toys and effects. Each department will have a lead elf, and your costumes will reflect which department you represent. You will be in charge of keeping your section in order, and most importantly, making it safe. We will be going through our Elf and Safety Policy after lunch,' she said, laughing at her own, extremely poor, dad joke. 'You will find your costume on a named hanger on the rail at the back…'

But before she had finished, everyone was off to look to see what department they had been allocated.

# CHAPTER 13

Shan was the first one to reach the clothes rail, like anyone was going to catch Lockley Lasses centre forward.

'Sports Elf,' she yelled, opening the cover with her name on, to find a bespoke black and white elf costume.

'Mr Renwick Junior requested that especially for you,' Pandora hissed through gritted teeth.

'Mr Renwick Junior,' Nana laughed. 'We're not in an episode of *Are You Being Served?* but I'd put money on Captain Peacock being in here somewhere.'

'Not to mention Mrs Slocombe and her you-know-what, Mary.' Norman let out a huge guffaw, while the rest of us just looked at the pair of them, clueless as to what they were talking about.

'I'll tell yous all later,' Norman chuckled,

tapping the side of his nose.

'Ooh, I hope I get to be Beauty Elf,' said Barry, arriving at the rail out of breath. 'Oh my God. I'm Haberdashery Elf,' he said, disappointment evident in his voice. He held up a costume which was covered in all kinds of crafting items. He would look like Widow Twankey! He popped on a wig in the shape of a big ball of bright red wool and stared at himself in the mirror. 'Anyone want to swap, if it's allowed?'

'I'll swap with you,' shouted Kitchen Elf, who had a colander on his head which was covered in tiny silver bells.

'Erm, thanks, but maybe I'll stick. You look like a Klingon!'

'No swapping,' Pandora grunted.

'What have you got, Nana Mary?' Shan shouted. 'Hurry up and get the cover off so we can have a look.'

There was an empty coat hanger inside Nana's cover with a big card attached.

*Dear Mary*

*Pandora will take you to the Alterations*

*Department where they will help you decide what kind of costume you would like – maybe no green face paint though! This is to thank you for the fabulous time I had as your dance partner.*

*Nate*

'We'll go up later today,' Pandora glowered. 'You made quite an impression on Nathaniel, Mrs O'Keefe... I mean Mary.'

'As you have made an impression on me,' Nana replied curtly.

'How come *she* doesn't have a department to look after?' Bathroom Elf shouted, a big silver tap wobbling on top of her hat.

'I'll be doing my bit, don't you worry about that, Netty Roll,' laughed Nana.

'And as for you, Mrs Claus,' Pandora continued, 'we thought you might just prefer to wear your own clothes, as we couldn't come up with anything more suitable than what you're wearing; although you'll find a supply of frilly aprons, as they will require changing regularly.'

'Ta,' I mumbled.

'I'd like to thank Nate. Where is he?' Nana

asked.

'Nathaniel doesn't involve himself in the grotto, other than on recruitment day. You won't see much of him.'

My heart plummeted into my big boat shoes.

'Which department does he work in?' I stuttered, desperate to be able to go and gawp at him from a respectable distance.

'Nathaniel doesn't have a proper role in Renwick's. He's in his last year of university, at Cambridge,' she boasted, 'but Sir Oliver insists that he works in the store during holiday periods, if he's at home – which he always is over Christmas.'

It sounds like Nate's dad and my mam would get on famously, sharing a common bond of forcing their offspring into hard labour.

'Nathaniel is usually in the Executive Office, or occasionally fills in on the shop floor if there's a need,' Pandora continued. 'But he won't be coming to work in the grotto.'

And I'm sure she muttered, *'I'll see to that,'* under her breath.

'Where's your *friend*?' I asked pointedly. 'The

Christmas Angel of the North? Why isn't she here with the rest of us?'

'Persephone has a dressing room to herself. She needs to ensure that she is fully in the zone for her starring role.'

'I know which zone I'd like to put her in,' Shan hissed.

'Okay, everyone, please take your costumes and get changed. Today is the official reveal of this year's grotto. You have fifteen minutes and not a second more. There will be a lot of very important guests there, and the media. Please be aware that you are not allowed to talk to them. If anyone asks questions, be polite and point them towards me.'

'Yes, ma'am,' Barry whispered, tugging his ball of wool like a forelock.

'We knows our place, yer ladyship,' Norman whispered. 'Heaven forbid we should actually converse with anyone la-di-bleedin'-da!'

Fifteen minutes later, we trooped behind Pandora through the store to the grotto entrance, all of us in costume except Nana. Two of Renwick's security staff dressed as Christmas wooden soldiers were on sentry duty at each side of the doors of the futuristic silver capsule, which would transport us, with the aid of AI, to Renwick's Mini Magical Shopping Land.

We piled in and took our seats on the little wooden benches. It was quite claustrophobic and very warm, especially for me in my padding, big woollen cardigan and scratchy wig, which made my head sweaty.

'I'm not sure I'm going to like this, Shan; you know I used to get travel sick. I hope it doesn't break down, us being the guinea pigs on its maiden voyage. We might get stuck in here,' I said, panic rising in me.

'It'll be mint, Don. It doesn't actually go anywhere; it's just pretend. You do know that don't you? I told you not to have those cold beans for breakfast,' she tutted.

The back door shut, and we were trapped. The capsule lights came on, and we could see it was like an aeroplane inside, with porthole windows that were actually screens. As the craft began to fire up for lift-off, the images on the portholes clicked on and were so very real that you would just think you were looking out of a window.

'Eeh, it's just like Alton Towers,' Barry squealed, clapping his hands together like a performing seal. Barry was almost as dramatic as Nana. Almost!

'I hate Alton Towers,' I whimpered through closed lips, scared to open my mouth in case of what might pop up.

*'This is Santa speaking.'*

A voice boomed out through the speakers making me jump, and I banged my head on the ceiling just for good measure.

'Oh no, it's not. I'm the real Santa, and I'm here,' Norman laughed. 'He's an imposter – we're being elf-napped!'

*'Get ready for take-off, children, and enjoy your special ride to Renwick's Mini Magical Shopping Land.'*

The sound effects increased, and the tin can began to shake violently, then seemed to be spinning around. I let out a blood curdling scream.

'LET ME OUT OF HERE!'

But it fell on deaf ears, as the others were all totally immersed in the experience, watching reindeer fly past the windows, big bright stars dancing in the night sky and magical lands with snow-capped mountains way beneath us as we flew over them. I know all this because Shan told me afterwards. I spent the entire three minutes of the journey, which felt more like three hours, with my head buried inside my capacious Mrs Claus handbag!

# CHAPTER 14

I fell out of the capsule and stumbled straight into the arms of none other than Nate Renwick.

'Oh, my word, Mrs Claus. Are you okay? Have you been putting Mary's green face paint on?' He smiled, and I thought that if I were to shuffle off this mortal coil right this very minute, I'd go happy. I clung onto him, as I was still very dizzy and just gazed at his four beautiful green eyes that were dancing in front of me.

'Donna, are you okay, mate? I thought you were joking,' said Shan as she came out of the capsule and took my other arm.

'Where are we?' I stuttered. 'This is not where we got on.' I gazed around at the most amazing festive scene in front of me.

Nate smiled. He was now back to having two sparkling green eyes that were catching the light from stars in the grotto ceiling, and they were mesmerising. I was starting to feel better, but maybe I needed support for a little while longer, so I clung on to his muscular arm, drinking in his amazing scent, which today was like taking a walk in a winter pine forest.

'Mrs Claus, the capsule just turns around 180 degrees, so you get out of the door at the other end, straight into Renwick's Mini Magical Shopping Land.'

I felt so stupid. 'It's my age,' I spluttered. 'I'm all of a dither, young man.'

Young man? What the heck was I saying? Maybe the bump on the head was more serious than I thought. Nate chuckled a little too happily for my liking, gently detaching his arm from my vice like grip.

'I'll leave you with Shania. Got to go and mingle but will see you all later. You take care, *old woman*,' he chortled, and strode off into the throng of guests who had arrived by more sedate means, like a lift or a staircase.

'Old woman,' Shan laughed. 'That's a bit rude, isn't it?'

'Suppose I have just called him young man, so that makes me rude too,' I replied, unwilling to believe that Nate Renwick could be anything other than perfect.

Just about fully recovered, I felt the colour return to my cheeks, then flush even further when I thought of Nate's firm biceps and how he probably had my fingerprints embedded into them like a tattoo – what I wouldn't give to find out if the rest of Nate Renwick was just as toned and honed as those arms!

Renwick's Mini Magical Shopping Land was amazing. It was like a Victorian Christmas market, with a main walkway and small open plan areas housing the various departments off to each side.

'Oh, look at my Mini Sports area!' shouted an excited Shan.

It was full of all kinds of toys relating to sport: dressing up kits, balls, games and even a tiny set of goalposts. The attention to detail was amazing. Barry was slightly less enthusiastic when he found Haberdashery.

'I know nothing about crafting,' he whinged when he saw the array of effects and activities in his area.

'Not to worry, Barry,' said Nana, 'I'll come and help you; I love a bit of fuzzy felting.'

'I suppose there are lots of sparkly things. I do like a bit of glitter!' he said, cheering up.

The place was buzzing with guests, and the press were floating about. This was a huge deal for Renwick's – it must have cost a fortune to design and bring the initial idea to the stunning reality that lay before us.

At the top of the market walkway sat three tiny cottages, each with a small front garden and white picket fencing. They were so cute. The sign on the one in the middle told us that this was Santa's Cottage. Norman ducked under the door and went and sat on his big red chair. Inside it was adorable; a real magical place to visit Santa Claus. Norman said it was the best grotto he'd ever had in all the years he had been working at Renwick's.

'Here's your chair, Mrs Claus,' he laughed, pointing to a rocking chair covered in a knitted throw.

'We'll find space for you too, Mary.' He looked at Nana with a twinkle in his eye.

Nana turned pink and patted her hair.

The cottage to the left was called Elves Cottage and was somewhere for us to dump stuff that we needed to bring with us from the green room. Disappointingly, it was just a normal shed inside. We made our way to the third cottage, and Nate came running towards us. The door was locked, and he handed me a key.

'You open up, Mrs Claus, because this cottage is for you.'

'For me?' I raised a grey stuck on eyebrow.

I put the key in the lock and pushed open the door. The inside was decorated as a cosy little sitting room, with one big chair to the side of a pretend fireplace. The cottage had bookshelves all around with loads of children's books, pens, pencils and even an old Typewriter on top of a tiny desk. There were floor cushions scattered across the festive flooring, and a Christmas tree twinkled in the corner. It was heaven!

'Mrs Claus, we decided we couldn't hide you away in the auditorium, so welcome to Storytime Cottage, from where you can do lots of storytelling across the day.'

I was speechless, and just nodded, feeling quite overcome. Maybe I needed to hang on to his biceps again – just in case!

Pandora bounded into *my* cottage – uninvited I hasten to add.

'Nathaniel, you're needed. The Christmas Angel of the North is about to make her appearance, and it's your job to accompany her around the guests.'

'I wondered where Per Una was,' muttered Nana. 'Suppose she's on a different contract to the rest of us.'

'Different planet, more like,' I sniped.

'I'd rather stay here with all of you,' Nate whispered to Nana, 'but needs must, otherwise Dad will be on my case.'

'Right, everyone to their workstations,' Pandora shouted. 'Get into character, smile and stay put until I come back and tell you otherwise.'

And she marched off, steering Nathaniel towards his fate.

# CHAPTER 15

I stood in the tiny cottage garden with Nana, and we watched the arrival of the Christmas Angel of the North, who was wearing the bog roll frock. It was stunning, but so wide there could have been a partridge in a pear tree living under there, and no one would ever have known.

'I'd have looked much better in that dress,' Nana tutted. 'She's got nowt up top – she's as flat as a witch's—'

'Nana!'

Nate was now wearing a dinner jacket and bow tie and looked like he could be in the running to become the next James Bond – I felt both shaken and stirred! He was holding Persephone's hand like he was allergic to her and doing his duty as heir to the Renwick empire without any great conviction. The pair, along with Pandora, drew parallel to Storytime Cottage as a television reporter approached and asked to do a 'piece to camera' with them.

'Absolutely,' said Pandora. 'Shall we stand in front of the cottage?' She ushered Nate and Persephone into the tiny garden and shoved Nana and me towards the door. 'You two make sure you keep out of shot,' she hissed. 'You're not in costume, Mary and well…' she looked at me and trailed off.

'With pleasure,' I snapped. She was really beginning to jangle my baubles, the woman was so irritating – like a posh version of Orange Morgan, minus the creosote.

We watched the proceedings through the tiny window. Pandora was fussing around Persephone, making sure her hair and makeup were perfect as the camera was setting up.

'Okay,' said the reporter, a woman I recognised who had been on our local news for years. 'Perhaps we can have you standing there together in front of the cottage door. I'll probably be asking the same questions you've been asked lots of times already today by other media outlets,' she laughed.

'That's a point,' I heard Nate say. 'I think this time we should try for a new angle. Mix it up a bit.'

'I'd appreciate that,' said the reporter. 'Always nice to have an angle that no-one else got.'

'Great!' You don't mind, do you, Percy?'

'Percy doesn't mind what?' asked Pandora, raising an eyebrow and looking increasingly concerned at how things were straying away from her carefully orchestrated format.

'That Percy steps away this time and makes way for a fresh approach,' said Nate.

Pandora and Persephone looked like they were having a competition to see whose eyes could stretch the furthest.

'But this might be our only television interview,' Percy whined. 'All the rest so far have been for social media. I'm the Christmas Angel of the North, the most important role in the grotto. Of course I should feature, shouldn't I, Pan?'

'You should,' Pandora stuttered.

Ignoring them, Nate yelled into the doorway of the cottage.

'Mary, Donna. Come out here please. I think we

need to show how Renwick's moves with the times and has introduced something new and different for this year.'

Pandora looked ready to explode.

'I'm not going out there, Nana,' I hissed. 'Look at the state of me. I'll never hear the end if half of Lockley sees me on the telly dressed like this. You go. You're always saying you were meant for stage and screen; well now's your chance. You've done stage recently, so here's your opportunity for screen. And you look lovely today. Is that a new coat?'

'Charity shop. It used to belong to Cissie Patterson, God rest her soul. She always had a fine taste in clothes.'

'Ladies, I can hear you nattering. Come on – let's get Renwick's on the telly!'

Nana exited from the cottage door like she was walking out of the Ritz.

'Mrs Claus isn't up to it,' she announced. 'She's still got jetlag from us getting here.'

'Has she flown in from the North Pole this morning?' asked Persephone seriously. Percy was not exactly the brightest pixie in the Christmas Forest.

Nana took her place next to Nate and very soon had everyone almost crying with laughter. All except the Ugly Sisters that is, whose pinched-up faces suggested they were probably planning how to get rid of both of us.

'Thanks so much, Mary,' said the reporter, when they eventually finished filming. 'That's the most fun interview I've done in ages. You're a natural. We must come back to follow your progress and do some mini features leading up to Christmas. I can't wait to see you in costume, and maybe you can do some Irish dancing for me next time?'

'Blooming love to, pet,' Nana smiled.

'See, Pandora,' said Nate looking smug. 'Sometimes a change is as good as a rest. Right Percy, you're back on. We've got Coast Link Radio next, so no need for any more of that glossy stuff you keep putting on your lips – no one's going to see it over the airwaves.' Nate smirked as he strode off towards the next interview.

# CHAPTER 16

Opening day arrived, and we piled into the green room. Nana had appeared on the local news the previous night, and we hadn't heard the last of it.

'Eeh, I look a bit like Helen Mirren, don't you think? I've definitely got the bone structure for the telly – I might get to be a one of them influency people when I get spotted—'

'Donna,' said Shan, interrupting Nana before we got chapter and verse. 'You don't have to come to work in costume; you can get changed when you get here.' She pulled on her black and white elf suit.

'I'm a method actor,' I said, like I knew what I was talking about. 'I need to stay in character.'

Truth was, I felt far more comfortable hiding behind my Mrs Claus persona – especially in front of Nate Renwick. Making a fool of myself as Mrs Claus was one thing, but as me – well that was another level of potential embarrassment entirely.

Nana disappeared up to Clothing Alterations to collect the costume she had planned, and the rest of us made our way to our workstations to face the day ahead. Norman was on his throne as I ducked into Santa's Cottage.

'Morning Donna, love. You ready for this? It's going to be hectic.'

'Ready as I'll ever be, Norman,' I said, sitting on my rocking chair next to him.

'Where's Mary?' he asked nonchalantly, but I could tell – Norman liked Nana!

'She'll be here soon – just gone to collect her costume. Did you see her on the telly last night?'

'I did, Donna. She's a fine-looking woman is your Nana. Has a bit of a look of Helen Mirren, don't you think?'

'You know she's my Nana?' I spluttered.

'Of course I do. Mary told me, but she also said to keep it to myself, and Santa never tells, so your secret is safe with me, Mrs Claus.'

I knew that Norman and I were going to get on just fine.

The first capsule 'landed' at three minutes past ten, and from that point on we didn't even have time to think. It was bedlam as we all tried to get to grips with our new roles in amongst the hustle and bustle of kids running around everywhere.

Nana appeared just in time for my first storytelling session at midday.

'Oh my God.' I looked at her, stunned by her choice of costume.

Nana had got her wish. She was the Angel of the North, but not quite the princess version she had so coveted. Nana's costume was a replica of the original sculpture, complete with wingspan that she controlled on strings so she could walk around without knocking people out!

'Donna pet, I longed to be the Christmas Angel of the North, so I did the next best thing. I'm the Angel of the North Elf. And very happy I am too.'

'You look fabulous, Mary,' Norman smiled. 'A true angel of the north.'

'Come on then, Mrs Claus,' said Nana, lowering her wingspan. 'Let's go and do your first session in Storytime Cottage.'

Pandora and Nate were at the door of the cottage as we went to open up. Nate burst into hoots of laughter when he saw Nana in her Angel of the North costume. Pandora, however, looked far less impressed.

'Mrs O'Keefe...' No Mary this time, I noticed. '...You were meant to be an elf that represented a department of the store. We already have our Christmas Angel of the North, and we don't need another one.'

'I disagree, Pan,' Nate grinned. 'What could be more representative of our great northern region than the real angel and Renwick's together. Mary, it's inspired.'

Pandora's face was looking far from angelic.

I took my seat and got my big book out. I had written a new, much shorter story for today's sessions, based on Renwick's Mini Magical Shopping Land and planned to keep freshening up the tales as I went. I hadn't expected Pandora to be there listening in, far less Nate, who had sat himself down on a cushion amongst the kids, who had been shepherded into the tiny room. I was feeling extremely nervous.

On the stroke of midday, I began to read, and like magic, once again, my nerves disappeared. The children miraculously managed to sit still and listen. Story finished, the cottage emptied. Everyone had seemed to enjoy it.

'That went well. Storytime is going to be a huge success, *Mrs Claus*,' said Nate, his green eyes twinkling like fairy lights. I could feel my pulse begin to beat faster than Rudolph's hooves.

'It needs more expression,' Pandora muttered. 'And perhaps you could maybe be a little, erm, less northern.'

I thought Nana was going to release her wingspan and knock Pandora out. I knew that look on Nana's face, so before she started giving Pandora a mouthful about how important it was to hold on to your working-class heritage, I steered her out of the door.

'Lunch time, Angel Elf. I'll consider your feedback, Pandora,' I lied, having no intention of doing anything that woman suggested.

'Mind if I join you both?' Nate grinned.

'I thought we were lunching together, Nathaniel, in the Executive Dining Room,' Pandora simpered.

'Nope, can't remember making any such arrangements, and they've got toad in the hole on in the staff canteen today. Come on, ladies – my treat. Suppose you can come too if you want, Pan, but probably not your thing.'

I was astounded when she agreed. Probably a case of keep your friends close and your enemies closer!

I shuffled behind them towards the canteen, and we sat at a table for four. Nana and Nate at once began to chatter like two old friends. Meanwhile, Pandora and I just sat silently, glaring at each other.

'Are you single, Nate?' Nana asked, in her usual, forthright manner.

I was just about to blurt out my usual 'Nana' then stopped.

'*Mary*, I'm sure Nate doesn't want to talk about his private life,' I croaked, but all the while hoping he would spill the beans.

'You and I for once actually agree on something, Mrs Claus,' Pandora snipped. 'That's rather personal and inappropriate, Mrs O'Keefe.'

'I don't have a problem with you asking, Mary. I'm very much single—'

Pandora looked crushed and let out a huge sigh.

'—but ready to mingle!'

Pandora immediately ditched the frown and beamed as brightly as the North Star.

'I have a lovely granddaughter,' continued Nana. 'She's single.'

Oh my God. She wouldn't, would she?

'You do?' Nate raised his eyebrow. 'Is she anything like Mary, Mrs Claus?' He turned, drawing me into the conversation.

'Erm, not really met her,' I said, shovelling in a huge chunk of sausage, thus rendering myself speechless.

'She's just like a younger version of me. Well, maybe a little more reserved,' Nana laughed.

'And what's she called, this single granddaughter of yours?' asked Nate.

I couldn't breathe, never mind chew the giant

sausage that was nearly blocking my airway.

'Maddie,' said Nana, quick as a flash. 'She's a university student like you. Newcastle.'

'Newcastle's a great uni. I would have liked to have gone there, had it not been for family tradition. Maddie is a lovely name; I hope you don't call her Mad for short?' he chuckled.

Did he know something? Surely not.

'You must get her to come into the store. Maybe she would like to hear one of Mrs Claus' stories?'

Pandora suddenly jumped to her feet, as if all of Santa's reindeer were chasing her.

'Nathaniel, we're late,' she said, making an exaggerated show of checking her watch. 'Come on – we need to get back to the office. Now!'

Nate finished the last bit of his Yorkshire pudding, winked at Nana and sauntered out of the canteen smiling.

# CHAPTER 17

The weeks flew by. We had all settled down into a routine and worked well as a team. It was the best fun, even though we were all exhausted by the end of each shift, due to the relentless queues.

Nana and Norman had taken to having little power naps in Storytime Cottage between performances – at least that's what they told me, and I didn't want to think about it in too much depth. Nana fulfilled her role in Renwick's with gusto and was loved by everyone in the grotto team – especially Norman it would seem!

Pandora was always around checking up on us, marching about like she owned the place, which I suppose she thought she might one day, if she could ever snare Nate Renwick. I sincerely hoped not. On the other hand, we hardly saw Persephone. She appeared in the grotto only when needed for a promotion, otherwise, word according to Barry the Oracle was that she was likely to be found in the Beauty Hall or the Personal Shopping section quaffing the champagne. When she did appear, she and Pandora would be glued together, cackling like the Ugly Sisters as they watched us work our bells off. I hope the Christmas Karma Fairy was ready to deliver them a suitable gift.

We didn't see too much of Nate either, much to my disappointment. He had been kept busy moving around the departments, filling in during the store's busiest period, but he did pop by from time to time to see us in Santa's cottage.

'You three look so cosy and peaceful in here,' he said as we got ready to face our second to last day of the season.

'Come back in ten minutes when the doors open, and it won't be quite so peaceful then,' Nana laughed.

'Have you all enjoyed working here?' Nate asked. 'Can't quite believe it's Christmas Eve tomorrow and our last day before all of this will be taken down. It will be like it was never ever here.'

'We've all loved it, haven't we, you two?' Nana looked at me and Norman.

'Best Christmas season I've ever had in Renwick's bar none,' Norman winked, looking at Nana.

'And you, Mrs Claus – I've heard on the grapevine that your stories have gone down really well and that the Library Service is hoping you'll continue some sessions for them after Christmas.'

'Erm, yes,' I blushed, hardly able to drag my eyes away from him. He was looking especially gorgeous today in a tight black tee shirt and black jeans. Mr Grey Street did casual very, very well!

'What department are you on today, Nate?' asked Norman. 'You're not your usual suited and booted self.'

'I hate that suit,' he smiled. 'I'm down in Court House Café, on the ground floor today – stupidly, someone decided it was wise to put me in charge of a coffee machine.'

Nate swung around. The back of his tee-shirt said 'Barista – You be the judge of our coffee!'

'I do like a double entendre,' I blurted out. 'Erm, being a writer that is,' I added quickly.

'I'm rather partial to them myself,' Nate

winked, looking me right in the eyes and, whoosh, I was nearly away off in Donna land where me and Nate were sipping our Espressos in the sunshine in St Mark's Square in, in… well somewhere in Italy!

Did you know it's Mrs Claus' very last story session today?' said Nana, interrupting my reverie. 'None tomorrow, it being Christmas Eve. Talking of which, Norman and I are looking forward to the Renwick's Christmas Ball tomorrow night.'

'Are you going too, Mrs Claus?' Nate asked.

'Erm, no. Got a date stuffing a Turkey,' I lied.

'I expect you have to attend, Nate,' Nana smiled. 'Have you got a partner? I might be able to help in that direction…'

My heart was beating somewhere in my throat as I glared at Nana, willing her to shut up.

'Of course he's got a partner, haven't you Nathaniel? We're going as a foursome with Persephone and Tristan,' Pandora said as she ducked through the door.

'Perhaps Mrs Claus needs my help with her turkey,' Nate smiled. 'Pandora, maybe you and I need to have a private chat.'

'Of course, Nathaniel. We can decide how to co-ordinate our outfits so we don't clash with Percy and Tris.'

Nate shook his head and followed her out of the cottage door.

\*\*\*

Talk in the staff canteen that day was all about the ball.

'Are you going, Barry pet? You can come with me and Norman if you like? Our Don… I mean Mrs Claus, is too busy pretending she needs to stuff a turkey, and Shania has a charity football match.'

'Thanks, Mary. Appreciate it, but I think I might have something else on.' He blushed.

'Something, or somebody, Bazza lad?' Norman raised an eyebrow. 'You were only whinging to me the other day that you hadn't met anyone for ages.'

Barry pulled the imaginary zip across his lips and threw away the key.

'That's for me to know and you lot to mind your own biz about!'

'Okay, son, no problem. But just shout if things change.'

Later that afternoon, it was time for my last story session. I felt really emotional as the children gathered to hear the last tall tale I'd be telling in Storytime Cottage. I'd written *When Santa got stuck in Renwick's on Christmas Eve,* especially for the occasion, and if I say so myself, it was as Christmassy as Santa Claus himself. I was just about to begin when Nate rushed into the packed tiny cottage.

'Couldn't miss your last one, Mrs Claus, especially as I hear it's about Renwick's.' He smiled *the* smile, and I thought I might just melt like a snowman in the sunshine. He was so nice to me, and Nana. Maybe Nate Renwick was just an old soul in a young body, who liked hanging around with golden oldies!

# CHAPTER 18

Christmas Eve. Our last day. Nana, Shan and I stood at the bus stop, full of mixed emotions. We were all agreed that Renwick's had been a brilliant experience, and that whilst we were looking forward to a rest, we would miss the gang and all the banter in the grotto. And, of course, I would miss seeing Nate Renwick. I don't suppose that even if I had met him as me, Donna Dobbs from Lockley, he would have been interested, but one could dream. I might just write a book about us. Perhaps a spicy romcom could be my next literary effort – my imagination knew no bounds, especially where it involved Mr Grey Street!

We piled into the green room. There was the usual round of greetings from the gang. Barry was especially chipper, his face glowing, a grin as wide as the Tyne.

'You look happy, Barry. Care to share?' I asked.

'Nope, but I expect you're going to find out soon enough,' he said mysteriously.

I knew that look. It was the same one I adopted when looking at Nate.

'You've met someone, haven't you?'

'Might have,' he shouted, doing a theatrical twirl, until he saw Pandora. As she entered the room, he literally stopped mid-spin, turned on his heel and bolted out of the door, passing her on the way. Pandora glared at him, and I swear, if looks could kill, Barry would be a heap of buttons and wool on the floor!

Pandora's face was as red as a holly berry, and her eyes looked like she was hanging Christmas stockings under them.

'Are you okay?' Nana asked. 'Are you allergic to something? You could try calamine lotion.'

'Yes, as it happens, I am allergic to something – you three. Oh, and that over-stuffed buffoon, Barry from the warehouse,' she said bitterly, looking at me, Shan and Nana.

For once, all three of us remained silent, which was a Christmas miracle in itself.

'Right,' she said, 'down to business, so listen up. It's our last day, and it couldn't have come quickly enough for me. My darling friend Persephone is unable to come in today—'

'Why? Has she got what you've got? Is it catching?' Nana asked, moving away.

'I'm not ill, Mrs O'Keefe, but if I had something, I'd gladly give you it.'

'I'm going to give you something in a minute, if you talk to Nana Mary like that again,' Shan fumed.

'Because Percy is indisposed,' Pandora continued without so much as a sorry, 'it means that there is no Christmas Angel of the North today, so we need someone to step up. It's Christmas Eve, and tradition is that the angel works alongside Santa Claus today, so I've got no choice but to appoint one of you lot. Seeing as neither you nor Boaty McBoatfeet over there,' she rudely pointed at Nana and me, 'have specific duties – which believe you me was not my choice – one of you can be the Angel of the North for today. You can thank me later, as it's probably the best thing that's happened to either of you all year.' Her face broke into a malevolent sly smile. 'I don't even want to imagine how ridiculous either of you will look in the dress, but so what. Nathaniel Renwick shouldn't have messed me about. If there are complaints, then he will have to deal with them, because I quit. If you need me, I'll be in Personal Shopping writing my resignation letter.'

Pandora was a woman scorned, that was for sure.

'Nate, or should I say Nathaniel, won't go to the ball with you, will he? That's what this is all about, isn't it?' I glowered at her. 'I've just about had enough of you and your insults. We have all worked so hard, and not a word of thanks comes from your lips. I've never met such a pair of pompous, privileged princesses as you and Persephone in all my life.'

'Don't suppose you have,' she sneered. 'That awful place you all come from won't exactly be brimming with class.'

'We might be from Lockley,' said Nana, 'but I've got more class in my bunion than you and the other Ugly Sister have between you. And listen up, before you get all uppity and tell me I can't say that – I don't mean how you look. You and that Percypony lass could both be beautiful young women, but ugliness comes from within. Seriously, pet, the pair of you need to change your ways or you're going to end up staying bitter and twisted, just like you are right now. Oh, and just for the record, no matter which of us wears that dress, we will look blooming fabulous. It might be hard for you to believe, but us Lockley lasses are even more privileged than you, because we are beautiful both outside and in.'

A cheer went up across the green room.

'You tell her, Mary,' shouted Kitchen Elf, banging a pan with a spoon.

'Boaty McBoatfeet,' Shan howled. 'Class! Now can I go and deck her? Joking, Nana Mary!'

'I knew this would happen when he insisted on hiring you three and fat Barry from the warehouse,' Pandora sneered, before bursting into tears and heading for the door.

\*\*\*

The elves all went off to their workstations, and Nana, Shan and I took a few minutes to collect our thoughts.

'Well, that was a bit full on to say the least,' I said, 'but what did she mean about Barry working in the warehouse? I thought he was from stage school.'

'Sweeping the stage, maybe,' Nana smiled.

'Anyway, every cloud and all of that. Nana, you're going to get your wish. You can become the Christmas Angel of the North like you always wanted, even if it is just for today. I wonder what's up with Persephone. Not that I really care, as the two of them deserve all they get.'

'Nana Mary, this is your chance. You deserve to go and sit with Norman looking like a queen, never mind a princess!'

'No, I can't,' said Nana.

'What do you mean you can't?' I gasped.

'I'm not staying – only came to show my face. I've got a pedicure, which I'm desperate for after weeks standing in here – me toenails are like reindeer antlers. Got to be at my best for the ball tonight, so much as it pains me, I can't be the angel. Donna pet, it's about time you got out of that ridiculous costume – I want to see my gorgeous granddaughter again. Not seen her in weeks.'

'No waaaaay. I am not wearing that dress. You do it, Shan; I'll be Sport Elf for the day.'

'Not a chance. I've got a five a side organised later this morning – Warehouse versus Security. Anyway, Nana Mary's right. It's time to get my bestie back, so I'm not taking no for an answer… It's Christmaaaaaas! Right, first things first, I'm going to find someone to cover for me for a little while, and then you're coming with me,' Shan said with determination. 'Say goodbye to Mrs Claus, Boaty McBoatfeet.'

# CHAPTER 19

Shan came back and thrust a white robe at me.

'Get your gear off, Mrs Claus. Hurry up, time's ticking – if I'm not there to referee it'll be mayhem.'

I hurried to the changing room and stripped away Mrs Claus. I had become quite fond of her, but it would be nice to ditch the padding. I removed the scratchy wig and my spectacles and placed them on top of my clothes.

'Better already, Don,' Shan smiled as I went back into the green room. 'But take those stupid shoes off.'

'I've not got any others to wear.'

'Oh, never mind, I'll sort that later. Come on, I want you to meet my new friend,' she laughed.

Shan marched me down to the Beauty Hall and made a beeline for one of the most expensive cosmetic counters in the shop. I couldn't even afford a free sample from there.

'Donna, this is Krystal. She's going to transform you,' said Shan, pushing me into a booth next to the counter and sitting me in a chair.

Krystal was as sparkling as her name suggested, and immediately got to work, sweeping off the last of Nana's make up that I had borrowed in an attempt to become a proper octogenarian. She opened a big drawer – it was a treasure trove of jewel like colours and glittery packaging, shining under the spotlights.

'Okay,' said Krystal standing back, hands on hips and looking at me like an artist might survey a blank canvas. 'What style are we going for Shania?'

'Here, don't ask her. She doesn't even wear makeup. How about the natural look?'

'Christmas Angel,' Shan said firmly. 'And don't listen to her. I'm in charge.'

'Icy and ethereal,' mused Krystal. 'Right up my street.'

She spun me around so I couldn't see in the

mirror and got to work.

Krystal finally laid down her magic brush, as she called it.

'Wow,' said Shan. 'Just wow. Donna mate, you look beautiful.'

'Can I look yet?' I asked, desperate to see the result. I'd seen plenty of makeover reveals on the telly, as Nana loved that type of programme, but she wasn't always complimentary about the results. Sometimes I agreed with her, which doesn't happen that often.

'One last thing before you do,' said Shan.

My hair had been in pins to hide it under the wig, so Shan removed them and teased her fingers through the long golden-brown strands which fell over my shoulders in waves.

'Perfect, like a fairytale princess. I knew me time in Shirley's salon wouldn't be wasted.'

Krystal spun the chair around and I looked at myself in the mirror. Well at least I think it was me. I had been expecting something totally over the top and tacky, but Krystal had achieved her aim of icy and ethereal quite subtly, with a lot of silver and sparkles, some amazing eyelashes that had tiny ice crystals on them, a flash of pink blush on a pale base, and a lick of iridescent lip gloss.

'It's lovely,' I said, quite overwhelmed.

'Is that it? Don mate, you could sound a little more excited. You look amazing.'

'Sorry, I think I'm in shock at the transformation. Krystal, I absolutely LOVE it, thank you so much. You're a miracle worker.'

'Yeah, thanks Krystal. Fancy a coffee next week, on Donna?' Shan laughed.

We went to leave the booth.

'Er, any chance of some free samples before we go? I could get used to using these premium products.'

'Donna, man!' said a horrified Shan.

'Well like Nana says, shy bairns get nowt.'

Krystal pushed a gauze bag full of mini treats into my hands, and her phone number into Shan's.

'Result,' Shan beamed.

Back in the green room, Shan took the frock down from its hanger and handed it to me.

'Off you go and put it on. I hope it fits after all of this.'

I kind of hoped it didn't, but I'd got this far so...

I came out of the dressing room, and Shan just stood looking at me, her mouth flapping open like a Christmas Carol singer mid tra-la-la.

'Oh my God. It's like it's not the same dress that Percy was wearing. Honestly, it really is magic, as it fits you like it was made just for you. It's sort of like the dress version of Cinderella's slipper I suppose—'

She was interrupted by Barry rushing into the room. When he saw me, he stopped dead on his heels and gawped, looking me up and down.

'Wow, who's...' Then his eyes alighted on the big boat shoes.

'Donna? Mrs Claus? Is that you? No waaay!' he squealed excitedly. 'You can't wear those things on your feet, though. What size do you take? And he rushed back out of the door, returning a few minutes later with a pair of dainty silver shoes.

'Don't ask – perk of the job,' he grinned.

'So we hear. You have a lot of explaining to do,

young Barry,' I croaked, reprimanding him in my Mrs Claus voice.

'Later,' he laughed. 'I just came to get Shan. Hurry up – we're all waiting. And make sure you give all those security guards red cards, otherwise we're going to get hammered!'

# CHAPTER 20

I almost floated across the grotto floor on my way to Santa's Cottage.

'Donna! Mrs Claus! Is that really you?' asked Bathroom Elf, making her way towards me through the hundreds of soapy bubbles the kids were blowing across her section. 'Is that a different dress?'

'Are you from an agency?' asked Kitchen Elf as I passed his area. 'Did Mary or Donna not want the job?'

'It is me, Donna,' I laughed. 'Mary was going to see about her feet, so I was, erm, persuaded – or should that be railroaded.'

'Well, I'm pleased you agreed, because you look absolutely fabulous, darling. Perfect for the role – unlike precious Percy. Who would have thought that under Mrs Claus' shapeless cardi lay a stunner like you?'

I blushed and hurried on.

As I ducked into Santa's Cottage, Norman was head down looking inside one of the gift bags.

'Sorry I'm a little late, Norman. Did Nana explain what was happening today?'

Santa slowly raised his head and looked up at me. He may have been hidden by enough facial hair to lend to the full cast of Game of Thrones, but there was no mistaking the bright green eyes that stared at me, unblinking.

'Na..Nate...'

'Do...Donna...'

'What the... How...' I stuttered. 'How did you know it was me?'

He didn't reply at once; he just continued to stare at me, his eyes looking extra green against the snow-white mass adorning his face. Then some of the facial fluff began to move, and I could tell that he had broken into a very wide smile.

'The eyes...' he eventually said.

'What eyes?' I replied. My concentration was

non-existent. I wondered if I had been somehow transported by that blinking AI capsule into a parallel universe.

'You asked how I knew it was you. It was your eyes. You should have had glass in those spectacles, because from the very minute we met and I saw your eyes peeping through those rims, I knew you were not only young but related to Mary. Hers are the same shade of cornflower blue. What I didn't know though was that an absolute angel was lurking underneath the frilly apron.'

'Mary's my Nana,' I said, feeling my face flush at his compliment.

'Yes, I kind of worked that out as we all got to know each other. Anyway, how did you know it was me under all this fluff?'

'It was your eyes too,' I murmured. 'They're remarkably green. All different shades, just like a kaleidoscope.' I gulped but continued to stare at him. Blue eyes met green, melted into a turquoise pool and locked into place. Neither of us seemed to have any desire to break away, or even blink.

'Donna, you look absolutely beautiful. The dress looks better on you than it has on any other angel, and there have been many across the years. Not all in my time though,' he laughed.

'You look lovely too,' I smiled, before realising what I had said out loud, but it broke the ice, as Nate burst out laughing, pointing to his baggy Santa Suit and facial shrubbery.

'Great, I know your type now.'

'It's like we've traded places,' I laughed. 'It's your turn now for the padding and a silly costume.'

I took my seat next to him, not quite believing that we were going to be side by side in this tiny cottage for the next few hours.

'By the way, do you know where Norman is?'

'Not sure. He came rushing down to the coffee shop and said he had to go somewhere urgently and that I needed to take over. I asked him why he hadn't gone to Pandora, but he said I was the only man for the job and that he wouldn't have just anyone as Santa Claus. Norman is very protective about his role. And where is Mary, er, your Nana Mary?'

'She said she had an appointment, but funnily,

she hadn't mentioned it before. Nate,' I smiled, 'I think we've been set up by the pair of them!'

'Fine by me,' he grinned.

'Fine by me, too. I can't even be annoyed at Nana for interfering this time.'

'What? Nana Mary interferes? I'd never have believed that,' he chuckled.

'Just a little bit,' I laughed.

'Right, here goes,' I said as the next child in the queue came barrelling towards us. 'Brace yourself.'

Nate was an absolute natural with the kids, and I felt my heart swell to bursting point as I watched how gentle he was with an extremely nervous little boy, who was quite out of his depth with the whole experience. I was longing for a break in the queue so that we might be able to talk to each other, but when the gap did come, it was quickly filled by a flushed faced Barry bursting into the cottage, followed by Shania.

'We had to come to see how you were enjoying being the angel. Doesn't she look stunning, Norman?' squealed Barry.

'Erm, it's not Norman,' I said. 'It's Nate.'

'It's who?' Shania asked, a confused look crossing her face.

Barry pulled down the Santa Claus beard.

'Yep, it's definitely Nate. What's going on?'

'Nana and Norman, that's what. Tell you later.'

Shania pulled me to one side of the cottage.

'I have no idea how Nana Mary swung this, but it's brilliant. Are you going to the ball with him?'

'Hey, you never know,' I smiled.

'I have news too,' Shan grinned, her face lighting up as brightly as the floodlights at her beloved St James Park.

'Quick, tell me,' I demanded.

'Krystal the makeup magician DM'd me. I'm meeting her on Boxing Day.'

'Woo hoo,' I shouted, throwing my arms around her and getting as close as the meringue frock would allow.

'See, I told you that it was a good idea us coming to work here. I was right, wasn't I? They say you're the bright one, but I have me moments!' Shan grinned.

'You absolutely do. Happy Christmas, bestie. Love you. See you tomorrow for dinner.'

'Happy Christmas, Don. Love you too. Remind your mam I hate those parsnip things – they're like the vegetable equivalent of Parma Violets. Right, Bazza, come on. Let's go and get you sorted for your big date.' Shania pulled Barry towards the door.

'What big date?' I asked, suddenly developing Barry's FOMO.

'Laters, Don,' said Shania. 'Your next customers are waiting.'

'Might see you at the ball tonight.' Barry winked at Nate, and then rushed off behind Shania.

'Ball?' He said he wasn't going. Wonder who he's going with?' I mused.

Nate started to laugh. Deep belly laughs, which made his beard flap.

'You mean you haven't heard?'

'No, heard what?'

'Erm, Pandora caught Barry in a bit of a compromising clinch in Elves Cottage, with none other than Tristan.'

'Tristan, as in Persephone's fiancé Tristan?' I gasped.

'Yep, the one and same.'

'So, she dumped him?'

'No, he dumped her. And now he's going to the ball with Barry, hence her having the hissy fit, not coming in today and threatening never to leave the house again. We should be so lucky.'

'And Pandora?'

'Let's just say I told her a few home truths, which she didn't appreciate. Pandora's father and my dad go way back, and she got the job here because of some kind of misplaced loyalty. She and Persephone will be okay – both as tough as Teflon. They'll probably go off to Chamonix after New Year and find some rich oiks to distract them.'

'Well, at least they can console each other over Christmas,' I said, momentarily wondering where Chamonix was.

Nana was right. She was always telling me what goes around comes around, and I mentally thanked the Christmas Karma Fairy who had indeed delivered the goods. It couldn't have happened to two more deserving cases.

# CHAPTER 21

Nate and I were kept busy all afternoon. Every time there was a slight break in the queue we turned and looked at each other, but before either of us could say a word, the next child was eager to meet Santa.

The store closed early on Christmas Eve. Just before we were about to shut the door of Santa's Cottage for the final time, in strode Nana and Norman. Nana stared at me and immediately felt in her pocket for a tissue.

'Eeh, Donna pet, look at you. See, Norman – Isn't she as beautiful as I told you she was?'

'Even more so, Mary,' nodded Norman. 'A younger version of you.'

'You don't look too shabby yourself, Nana,' I said, taking in her floor length sequinned evening gown. 'That's a beautiful dress.'

'Another of Cissy's,' she winked. 'Her best cruise frock.'

'How are your toenails?' I asked seriously.

'My toenails?' Nana looked confused. 'Oh yes, those toenails. Sorted.' She smiled sheepishly.

'Nate, you make a grand Santa Claus, lad,' Norman grinned. 'Am I in danger of not getting my job back next year?'

'I don't think so, Norman, although it has been one of the best afternoons I've ever had in Renwick's,' Nate smiled, looking at me. 'Anyway, you don't look half bad yourself, Sir Norm. That's a dapper evening suit you've got on.'

'Don't tell anyone, especially Pan Handle, but I've borrowed this from the shop dummy in Menswear.'

'Your secret is safe with Santa,' Nate laughed.

'Anyway, you two, have you got anything else you want to tell us?'

'Don't know what you mean, Donna pet. We just thought we would pop in to say hello. We're off for Christmas cocktails before the ball. I'm desperate to try Sex in the Snow.'

'Nana!'

'Will we see you at the ball later?' asked Norman.

Nate just grinned and said nothing.

'I've got that turkey to stuff, remember?' I said quickly, beginning to appreciate how Pandora must have felt not getting an invite.

Nana and Norman left for the cocktail bar, and only then did I realise that nothing was stirring outside Santa's Cottage. I went into the tiny garden and what lay before me was an abandoned Renwick's Mini Magical Shopping Land. Everyone had gone, rushing off to do their own last minute Christmas preparations, no doubt.

'Well, that's a wrap,' said Nate, joining me in the garden. 'It really has been the most fabulous Christmas event we've ever had.'

'You can take your fluff off now.'

'It's only Christmas Eve, so I can't take it off yet. I'm still technically on duty. Donna, I wanted to ask you something—'

'Is this Santa or Nate speaking?' I asked.

'Most definitely Nate. Donna, I wondered if you

would like...' he faltered, 'erm to go—'

'No, I'm not going to the ball with you.' I jumped in before he had finished. 'That would be far too predictable. This isn't a version of Cinderella where the Ugly Sisters get their comeuppance, Nana Godmother waves her magic wand and poor old Cinderdonna from Lockley gets to go to the ball with the handsome Prince.'

'You think I'm handsome?' His eyes crinkled at the corner in a smile. 'Actually, I wasn't going to ask you to go to the ball.'

'You weren't?' My face flushed as scarlet as Nate's suit. Sometimes I just wish my mouth would learn to remain shut. Another unwanted genetic trait I'd inherited from Nana. 'Sorry, my mistake,' I said as I turned to walk towards the green room, embarrassment seeping through me all the way to my toes.

'Donna,' he shouted after me. 'Why on earth would I ask you to a stuffy ball where everyone would take up the time that I could spend alone with you so that we can get to know each other. I'd hardly get the chance to see you. It would be torture just like this afternoon's been, being so close to you yet hardly able to speak to each other for interruptions.'

'Oh, I see.' I murmured, feeling even more embarrassed. 'Sorry, I promise to keep my trap shut this time, so whatever it is, ask me again – please.'

'Donna, I wondered if you would like to help me to get Lost in Lockley? I am Santa, after all, and it's Christmas Eve. Let's have some fun recreating your story. You can take me to some of those hilarious places you read to us about at your audition. Tell me about your life, what you wish for, whether you like Brussels sprouts – all that kind of stuff.'

'Lockley? Are you mad?' was all I could stutter.

'Maybe just a little. That's a trait I've inherited from my very dysfunctional mother. What do you say? Next time, we'll do my place, although it doesn't sound half as interesting.'

Next time. He was already mentioning a next time!

'Is that a yes?' he said, holding out his hand.

'It most certainly is,' I said, reaching

out towards him. The moment I clasped his hand, a power surge that would ignite every single Christmas light on Northumberland Street whooshed through my body.

'Come on then,' he said, pulling me away from the grotto towards the capsule of death.

'One last time for good measure?' he nodded at the silver machine.

'Not even for you, Nate Renwick. Now press the button on the lift.'

We went down to the basement car park. Nate spoke to the security guard, who went into a small office and handed him a set of keys.

'Ooh, are we going in style or on your sleigh?'

Nate laughed.

'I haven't got a sleigh, me being a temporary Santa, but I do have the next best thing.' He walked towards the Renwick's vintage delivery van that they only used at Christmas. It was adorable, with green and gold livery and tiny fairy lights hanging up inside.

'No way,' I laughed. 'If we turn up in Lockley on Christmas Eve in this, dressed like Santa and an angel, they'll think that Beryl Balls has been tinkering with her cookies again! It's like something out of Beamish.'

It was already dark, and the stars had started peeping out in the clear inky blue night sky, when we negotiated our way through the city traffic in the little boneshaker of a van. Nate knew his way around town, and before too long I realised we were about to head over the Tyne Bridge.

'Nate, Lockley isn't over the river. You'll have to turn around.'

'All will become clear. We're just going on a little diversion first.'

He drove on for a couple of miles, then pulled into an eerily quiet car park next to the main A1 motorway, turned off the engine and jumped out of the van. There ahead of us, standing majestically on the top of a slight incline, was the iconic Angel of the North.

'I thought it would be fun for my Christmas Angel of the North to meet the other Angel of the North,' he grinned, grabbing my hand and pulling me up the bank towards the sculpture.

We were the only two people there. Maybe

everyone else was just too busy on Christmas Eve to stand in the freezing cold looking out across the spectacular landscape of urban Tyneside, lit up by a million orange lights.

'This view is special, isn't it? said Nate. 'I love seeing the angel every time I come back from university. I know I'm nearly home, and now it'll also always remind me of you.'

My heart warmed to the point of becoming tropical, but the rest of me was freezing.

'It's perishing,' I said, shivering as I gazed at the angel's enormous wingspan, which seemed to be catching the first few snowflakes of winter.

Nate wrapped his arms around me, and I snuggled into his cosy costume, breathing in his festive spiced scent. I gently pulled down his beard and gazed at his face, thinking that I had never seen anyone quite as handsome. As he pulled me towards him for our first kiss, I glanced up at the towering figure looking down on us, and I swear there was a nod of approval from one angel to another. As my lips met Nate's, I couldn't help but think this was one Christmas story that really did have a very happy ending!

# AFTERWORD

If you have made it this far then hopefully you have finished the book - and I really hope you enjoyed it. You can support authors by leaving a star rating or if you have time, a written review on Amazon.

Writing about Donna, Nana Mary and the supporting cast was such a joy. They made their debut in a Comedy Women in Print Competition and were screaming at me to release them from the laptop again and I was only too happy to oblige!

So, what happens next from the little writing room of me, Kimberley Adams? I'm not sure Nana,

Donna and Shania are ready to go back to a quiet life in Lockley just yet so...

*When Donna inadvertently gets the entire Lockley Knit and Natter group ga-ga on Beryl Balls questionable Canni Biskits, her penance is to organise a trip for them all to an 80's week at a run-down holiday park in Whitley Bay...whatever could go wrong! Free spaces on the coach if you fancy the ride!*

*Or perhaps we should pop back to Lindisfarne and see what Zen and Ellie are up to? Might there be a weddding to orgainise? What might the tide bring in...*

To find out just where we might go to next, follow me on social media. Info listed at the end.

Love and stotties
Kim

# THANK YOU...

To the ever patient Jo Mabey, a friend and fellow member of Northumbrian Writers Group who painstakingly edited this book. Jo, I truly cannot thank you enough.

To Sarah for once again producing the most darling cover, and to Rachel for adding the final touches of magic.

For all the continued help and support I get from the reading and writing communities on social media - without you these book things just wouldn't happen and I am eternally grateful.

# PRAISE FOR AUTHOR

*Kim's first book, Love Lindisfarne, has hundreds of amazing reviews on Amazon from lovely readers who have enjoyed the book. One called it a Love Letter to the North which I think sums it up perfectly!*

*Love Beyond Lindisfarne is one of the highest rated romantic comedies on Amazon. The follow up to Love Lindisfarne , LBL was selected as a featured romance in this year's Amazon Storyteller competition (2024) Read the amazing reviews on Amazon from the lovely readers who enjoyed the book!*

# BOOKS BY THIS AUTHOR

## Love Lindisfarne

Take a Christmas trip to magical Northumberland and find love amongst the stars in this feelgood romantic comed, which will transport you to iconic Holy Island where dreams really can come true!

## Love Beyond Lindisfarne

Take a spring to summer trip to magical Northumberland and find love and laughter in this feel-good romantic comedy which will transport you to the iconic island of Lindisfarne and beyond...

# SOCIAL MEDIA LINKS

**Facebook**

Kimberley Adams - Writer

Love Lindisfarne

**X TWITTER**

@kim_adamsWriter

**INSTAGRAM**

Kimberley Adams - Writer

Join me, I'd love to see you there for some banter and keeping you up to date with happenings from the little writing room.

Printed in Great Britain
by Amazon